# At the Corner of Rock Bottom & Nowhere

L.A. WITT

ISBN-13: 978-1544145570
ISBN-10: 1544145578

# Copyright Information

First Edition.
Copyright © 2017 L.A. Witt

Cover Art by Lori Witt
Editor: Jules Robin

ISBN-13: 978-1544145570
ISBN-10: 1544145578

# AT THE CORNER OF ROCK BOTTOM & NOWHERE

# Chapter 1
## Adrian

Las Vegas is a weird place. I've never lived anywhere else, but I've traveled a little and I've seen enough movies to understand that this electric desert oasis isn't like other cities. It isn't just the Strip, either, or the fact that other places apparently don't have slot machines at the airport or poker machines at 7-11.

There's a different vibe here. Or…two vibes at once, I guess. Like two parallel worlds existing in the exact same spot on two different planes, completely unaware of each other.

The one most people know about—and the reason they come here in droves for vacations—is the shiny, sparkly one. The Las Vegas that always makes it into the movies, where it's nothing but glittering lights, jingling slot machines, cheering crowds around craps tables, and drive-thru wedding chapels.

The other Vegas sucks. It's the gritty, gross part. The burnt-out lights, the losing slot machines, the depressed tables where no one is winning, and the quickie divorces. It's seeing the same person at the same slot machine or the same table at ten in the morning in the same clothes they were wearing when you saw them at midnight. There are pawn shops filled with wallets, cell phones, jackets, shoes, jewelry—the last few meager possessions a person unloads in the name of scoring a few dollars. Sometimes they're smart and use that handful of money to get on a bus and hightail it out of town. Or if they don't have enough for that, at least go to one of the buffets and get something to eat.

But usually, the money winds up in a predictable place—a casino's coffers.

Sooner or later, people run out of things to pawn, and they wind up huddled against a wall with nothing but the clothes on their back and a sign scrawled on a wrinkled piece of cardboard. Nobody sees them, but they're here, all along the Strip—the destitute people who've given their last dime to the casino gods and have nothing left. No money. No way out.

I live in that gray area between the two parallel worlds. Too jaded to be won over by the sparkly shit. Too numb to pay attention to the sad underbelly.

I walk down the Strip every day and every night. I step over the odd pool of vomit, get nearly run over by drunken partiers having the time of their lives, and pass by the still, sad homeless people without even looking long enough to read their cardboard signs. Once in a while— usually after I've watched someone lose everything at my blackjack table—I feel guilty enough to drop a handful of change into their cup. Especially when they're using those plastic coin cups from the casino where I work.

But I don't meet their eyes and don't really give them much thought. As soon as the coins clang in the bottom of the otherwise empty cup, I've done my part, and that's the end of it. I walk on and ignore them like I do all the other sad realities of this town.

Tonight as always, I want nothing more than to get home and take a shower. After six hours of dealing cards, I danced for another four at the NightOwl. My feet hurt. My body is exhausted. Nothing exists for me now except fatigue and the promise of a hot shower and several hours of sweet, sweet sleep.

Hands tucked in my pockets, I weave through the crowd outside the Bellagio. The fountains are dark and quiet this time of night—the water-and-light shows stop sometime around midnight—but there's a reason they call this the city that never sleeps. Most people on the sidewalk are swaying a bit. Some drunk. Some probably just tired as hell. It's Sunday night, after all—well, early Monday morning—so a lot of the weekend revelers are running out of steam.

The railing along the Bellagio's enormous fountain has little patios every few feet for people to stand and watch without blocking foot traffic. Not that they're big enough to accommodate everyone who wants to see the show. When the fountains are going, it's a nightmare to walk through here.

It's not so bad now, and as I pass one of the patios, there's a homeless man pressed back up against a concrete planter. He's a typical sight—rumpled clothes. A cardboard sign. A plastic cup.

I glance at him with the same interest I might glance at a manhole cover or some graffiti and keep walking.

For about eight feet.

I halt abruptly enough that a group of women—one wearing a tiny telltale white veil—crash into me, nearly knocking me off my feet. Someone slurs an apology, and then they're gone, staggering down the walkway toward the next bachelorette party destination.

My feet are under me again, but I don't start walking.

I glance back at the homeless guy. He doesn't see me. His head's down, and I wonder if he might be asleep or passed out. There aren't any bottles near him, aside from an empty Aquafina bottle lying by his foot, though maybe he's got something in the backpack tucked up against his leg. I didn't smell any alcohol on him, but I've been inhaling cigarette smoke all day, and my nostrils were pretty much seared by the booze radiating off my last lap dance customer of the night.

He's wearing a suit. It's hard to tell for sure in the dim light, but it looks expensive. Finely cut. A nice gray material. I'm no expert, but I doubt those shoes are cheap. Wherever this guy fell from to land here—on the street outside the Bellagio with a cardboard sign at two o'clock on a Monday morning—it was a lot higher than any place I've ever been.

Poor guy.

Shaking my head, I continue walking. I try to think ahead to shower and sleep, but something tugs my mind back to the homeless guy in the suit and nice shoes. Ridiculous. He's hardly the first person I've seen who went from high-rolling to begging for change. He'll hardly be the last.

And yet, with every step I take, guilt burrows deeper into the pit of my stomach.

My feet slow without any conscious effort on my part. Then, once again, I stop. This time it's not such an abrupt halt, and nobody crashes into me, though some shitfaced guys just barely miss.

I stand there for a long moment, hemming and hawing, before I finally turn around and backtrack.

He's still there. In the moments since I walked by him, someone's dropped a winkled bill into the cup. Or maybe it was there before and I just didn't notice it. He's awake, too, but looks out at the dormant fountain instead of at the people passing him by. I wonder how many people he walked by before he crashed and burned too.

After a moment, he tenses a little, and turns toward me, like he's just realized there's someone standing here. He lifts his chin, and a pair of dark, exhausted eyes meet mine. Then he breaks eye contact and pulls his knees in close to his chest. "Am I in your way? Sorry."

In my way? It's weird—and makes me feel guiltier—that he's worried he's in the way. I'm used to stepping around homeless people. I didn't even have to step around him because he'd situated himself outside the flow of traffic.

"You're not in the way," I say quietly.

He looks up at me again, but keeps his knees hugged to his chest. His jaw is scruffy, a few gray hairs peppering the otherwise dark beard. My guess is it's been three or four days since he's shaved, so whatever happened to all his money—whichever casino, hooker, or drug dealer took the last of it—it wasn't all that long ago. Something about him is familiar, but I can't put my finger on it. And anyway, I see countless faces every day, either at my blackjack table or when I'm dancing.

And he's still watching me, equal parts curious and uneasy about my sudden fascination with him.

*Yeah, I'm right there with you.*

I clear my throat. "You, um…" I scrabble for words, and finally settle on gesturing up the road and saying, "There's a twenty-four hour buffet up there. If you want something to eat, I can buy you a plate."

His eyebrows jump, and the way his jaw works, I suspect his mouth is watering. Still, he stays guarded. "Why?"

"Because I'm going to guess you haven't eaten in a while."

His eyes flick toward the Aquafina bottle. There's a Snickers wrapper next to it. Either some litter that blew up next to him, or the remnants of a small act of kindness from a passerby. Or hell, maybe he stole it. Or scrounged up enough change to buy it.

Returning his gaze to me, he keeps his voice flat and disinterested. "You don't even know me."

"No." I swallow. "But…" I can't think of anything that doesn't sound patronizing. "The offer's open. You don't have to."

"Neither do you."

L.A. WITT

I want to be frustrated with him, but I suspect I'd be just as reluctant if I were in his position. Pride, for one thing. Also because in this town, a lot of things have strings attached.

"No strings," I say. "I'll help you get something to eat, and then I can drive you down to the shelter. It's…gotta be better than sleeping on the sidewalk."

He gnaws his lip, considering me uncertainly. "I don't have any way to pay you back."

"It's okay." A casual comment about how it isn't much almost makes it past my lips, but I stop it in time. Yeah, a little bit of gas and two plates at a buffet isn't a lot of money for me, but that might be kind of insulting from someone with a few dollars and a handful of change to his name.

"Are you sure?" he finally asks.

I nod. "Yeah."

"I'm, uh…" He looks down at himself, then shyly back up at me. "I'm not really presentable to go into a restaurant, am I?"

I smile. "It's Vegas. They've seen worse." I flinch at my own comment, realizing a second too late that I sounded like a dick.

But he actually cracks a little laugh, and shrugs. "Okay. Um, I've got…" He pats his backpack. "If they don't mind me using their restroom, I could actually clean myself up. You know, get rid of this." He strokes his beard and wrinkles his nose.

"I don't see why not."

"All right. Well…" He releases a long breath, and gathers his things—the backpack, the change cup, the sign, the bottle and wrapper—and stands. At his full height, he's got at least three inches on me. Not that that's a shock since I'm only five nine in boots.

He shifts his weight. "I didn't catch your name."

"Adrian. Yours?"

"Max." He extends a hand but then starts to retreat, as if he's second-guessed the idea.

I clasp it, though, and shake it. "Let's go get something to eat."

"Let's?" His eyebrow lifts. "You're joining me?"

"If I'm going to drive you to the shelter afterward, I might as well."

"Oh." His eyes flick down.

So do mine.

We haven't let go of each other's hands.

Abruptly, we do, and he mutters something like "Give me a sec." Then he steps away to tuck the bottle and wrapper in a trash bin, empties the contents of the cup into his hand, and pockets the meager sum before putting the cup and sign into his backpack.

While Max goes through those motions, I take in a few more details. He's broader in the shoulders than I am, but most guys are. There's a stain across his shirt and blue tie, like he dumped some coffee on himself. Or, judging by where it is—starting mid-chest and splattering up his shoulder—like someone threw one on him. No wonder he's wary of me.

With his pack on his shoulders, he faces me, and he struggles to hold my gaze. "I really appreciate this. Most people just walk by."

The guilt in my gut burrows deeper. *I'm usually one of those people,* I don't say. *And I don't know why I didn't this time.*

But I just nod in the direction I'd been walking earlier. "It's, um, a couple of blocks this way."

"Thanks," he says again, and we start walking.

# Chapter 2
## Max

The last few days have made me more wary of strangers than I've ever been in my life. The sheer vulnerability of living—if you could call it that—on the street is terrifying. I'd admittedly turned up my nose at the homeless in the past, but I'd never thought about what it might be like to be one. It had never occurred to me that someone might offer me a cup of coffee, then toss the scalding hot liquid on me and laugh with their drunken idiot friends before wandering off. I also never realized how cold the desert gets at night until I had to sleep outside in a wet shirt.

It's been a hell of an education.

So when Adrian stepped away from the endless stream of people and offered to help me out, I was nervous. He seemed genuine, though. There was pity in his eyes, which made my pride want to shrivel up and die, but nothing about him struck me as threatening or malicious.

Ten minutes or so after I joined him, we walk into one of the casinos. It's not one of the giant ones that are visible from space. Not the Luxor or Caesar's Palace. It's smaller and smokier, with lights that aren't quite so bright and slots that don't seem quite so loud. Or maybe that's just because it's so late at night. I don't even know what time it is.

There's a small line out the door of the buffet. Typical Vegas. And I've heard that's a good sign, anyway. You don't want to go into a buffet that doesn't have a few people waiting. If there's no line and the place is deserted, there's probably a reason for it.

A few feet shy of the line, Adrian stops. He gestures at a sign above the walkway. "The signs will take you to the restrooms. I'll wait for you here."

"Thanks." I give him the best smile I can muster, then follow the signs. I'm tempted to look back and make sure he hasn't had second thoughts and run out the door. At this point, even if he has, it's not all bad—at least I'll finally get to clean myself up a bit.

All the way to the men's room, no one gives me a second look, and I wonder why I didn't do this sooner. I'd dashed in to use the casino restrooms a few times when nature called but hadn't dared take the time to fix myself up. I'd been convinced they'd throw me out, but now that seems stupid. How would they know?

Then again, I remind myself as I push open the heavy door, I'm new to being homeless. I don't know how all this shit works.

The restroom is deserted. I slip into a stall and open my backpack. I have three sets of clothes left to my name, and the two in the bag are clean. With no place to get dressed without risking a public indecency charge, and no way to do laundry, I'd been reluctant to change clothes until I absolutely had to. Of course now I realize I could have gone into a casino like I'm doing now. And hell, maybe a public indecency charge would've been enough to send me to jail. At least then I'd be indoors and have something to eat.

I really do suck at being homeless.

Once I've changed into a pair of jeans and a T-shirt, I leave the stall and park my bag at my feet in front of the sinks. I dig out my toiletry kit and get to work. Shaving, putting on deodorant, washing my face and hands, brushing my teeth—I'm pretty sure I will never again take for granted how good these things feel. Whenever I made it home or to a hotel after a long flight, I'd loved scrubbing away the grossness of traveling and making myself look presentable again. That has *nothing* on how amazing it is to de-scruff myself after almost a week on the streets of Las Vegas.

When I'm finished shaving, I splash some more water on my face. A few drops land on my T-shirt, but I don't care. It'll dry, and anyway, it isn't scalding hot coffee.

I stuff the toiletry kit back into my bag, then face the mirror. It's kind of like seeing another me. One who doesn't exist anymore. Cool and confident, well-groomed and standing in front of an ornate backdrop, even if it's just the gilded décor of a goddamned casino restroom. Staring down that version of myself, I can almost make myself believe I imagined the last several days and the even darker days before that. Almost. Maybe if I weren't wearing Italian leather shoes with a pair of jeans, and I weren't looking gaunt enough that my mother would throw a fit if she were still alive.

*I'm* still alive, though. That's something. Don't know what I'm going to do with it, but it's something.

I hoist my bag onto my shoulders and step out into the casino.

As the buffet comes into view, so does Adrian. He's looking at his phone, so he doesn't know I'm looking at him. And really, this is the first time I *have* looked at him.

Turns out he's exceptionally good-looking. He's dressed in form-fitting black jeans and a snug T-shirt with a pair of lazily tied and very faded Converse sneakers. Black hair tumbles into his eyes enough that he's constantly brushing it away, and in the back, it just teases his collar. I've never been a fan of long hair, but I can make an exception for him, especially the way it frames his slim face that's somehow both smooth and angular.

L.A. WITT

Despite living in the desert—at least, I assume he lives here—he's fair-skinned. Not pasty or pale, but fair. I'm not sure what color his eyes are. Suddenly I want to know.

He's familiar, too, though I'm not sure why. From the way he stands and moves—it's all with an effortless grace that I've always loved in a man—I wonder if he's a dancer of some sort. There's no shortage of them in this town. As lithe as he is, with that tight black T-shirt clinging to some slender but obviously powerful muscles, I wouldn't be surprised if he's part of one of the Cirque du Soleil shows.

As I come closer, he lifts his gaze from his phone and zeroes right in on me.

Blue. His eyes are blue. Vivid, ice crystal *blue*.

He's got on a little bit of black eyeliner, too. Smudged and smoky and unavoidable. I'm not sure how I missed that before, but I definitely see it now.

He smiles, nodding toward the buffet. "Ready?"

My focus immediately shifts from my beautiful savior to the restaurant, and my mouth starts watering just like it did when he'd suggested the idea. "Yeah. Definitely."

We stand in line, but not for long. In minutes, we have a table, I have a plate in my hand, and there's so much food laid out in front of me, I want to cry. In the last three days, I've consumed a grand total of the two granola bars I'd had in my backpack, a sandwich from an exceptionally kind passerby, and a Snickers bar I bought with some of the change I'd collected. Standing here like a fool in front of all these endless arrays of food, I don't even know where to start.

Adrian appears beside me, also holding a plate. "We can stay as long as you need to. So don't feel like you have to inhale it all in five minutes."

I just nod. The hunger that's been consuming me for days is so intense now, it's excruciating. Still, I'm vaguely aware that I should go easy at first. No point in making myself sick.

18

I walk through the buffet twice, getting just small portions of a few different things before returning to our table. It's a weird feeling, walking away from food. All it took was just shy of a week for me to develop that instinct to not let a single morsel pass me by because it might be the last thing I eat for a while. I'm still edgy, carrying my modest plate to the table and boldly taking for granted that the buffet won't magically evaporate while my back is turned.

A waitress comes by for a drink order. I order an ice water and cautiously ask if she can just bring an entire pitcher to the table. Moments later, she does.

Adrian sits across from me. We eat in silence for a little while. Now and then, our eyes meet, and there's still pity in his, but something else too. Curiosity, maybe? That must be it. I swear I can see the giant question mark hanging over his head. I'm terrified he's going to ask how I wound up on that sidewalk, and I suppose he has every right to. I just don't know how much I want to dive into it. The shame burns hot enough even without explaining what happened.

After my second plate, I don't go back right away. I suspect I'm not anywhere near finished, but with as little as I've eaten lately, I'd better pace myself.

Sitting back in my chair, I sip my water, wondering if water has always tasted this good. If anything has.

I idly swirl the water like a fine glass of wine. "Two weeks ago, I had dinner in a Michelin-starred restaurant. Had a three-hundred-dollar steak." I push out a breath and meet Adrian's eyes. "And I swear to you, it didn't taste nearly as good as this buffet shit does."

He laughs, and I love the way his lips curve when he does. "There isn't much that tastes bad when you're really hungry."

"Yeah. I'm learning that real fast."

Then we're silent again, and I can feel the question in his eyes. Now he's really curious, and it's my own damn fault for bringing up the steak.

He watches me. I watch him. The eyeliner isn't the only thing darkening the skin around his eyes. There are some definite circles there. He must be exhausted.

I glance around, then remember casinos don't have clocks. "What time is it, anyway?"

Adrian pulls out his phone. "Almost three thirty."

"That explains a lot." I glance around the sparsely crowded restaurant. "Do I even want to know what day it is?"

"Monday. The fourteenth."

I whistle before I take a deep swallow of water so cold it makes my teeth ache. I don't want to explain it to him. Why the days have all blurred together and I'm a human trash fire. I feel good right now, and I'm not ready to feel like shit again.

Clearing my throat, I set the glass down and face him. "So you live here? In Vegas?"

He nods but offers nothing more.

"How long?"

"All my life." He absently traces lines in the condensation on his glass with his long fingers. "I was actually on my way home from work when I…" His eyes flick up to meet mine. "When I ran into you."

"Oh. What do you do?"

He regards me silently, as if he knows I'm avoiding the elephant in the casino. If he does, he lets it go, at least for now. "I'm a blackjack dealer." Pause. "And a stripper." His eyes are locked on mine, and he lifts his chin just slightly, as if challenging me to have an issue with it.

"Oh. Funny—I thought you must be a dancer of some sort."

His black-lined blue eyes narrow a little. "Why's that?"

"Just the way you move. Dancers have a certain…" I wave a hand because the word just won't come to me. "I don't know. Grace, I guess?"

That softens him a bit. He relaxes against his chair, and I think he even blushes. I'm not sure what to say.

Then he asks, "So where is home for you?"

*Here we go.*

"Is that an icebreaker before asking how the fuck I wound up on the streets?"

A faint smile forms on his lips, and he lifts a slender shoulder in a half shrug. "It doesn't have to be. I'm just curious where you came from."

I reach for my drink, and mutter into the glass, "A gilded cage at the top of an ivory tower built on sand."

Adrian's eyes widen, revealing just how blue they really are. "Oh."

Sighing, I set the glass back down. "I'm sorry. It's…just a really long and depressing story."

"You don't have to tell it." He pauses. "I guess I'm just curious where you'll go after this."

*After this.*

*Where I'll go.*

*Where* will *I go?*

*What* does *come after this?*

*Oh my God.*

I stare at my empty plate for a moment and realize I'm still fucking starving.

"I'm, uh…" I stand and gesture at the buffet. "I'm going to do another round."

And then I go before he can say anything else.

L.A. WITT

# Chapter 3
## Adrian

I watch Max return to the buffet, and I don't know what to make of him. Whatever put him on the street is obviously a raw nerve, so I'll leave it alone despite my burning curiosity.

As he stands at the soup station, bowl in hand while he looks from one giant pot to the next, I study him. He looks so different now that he's cleaned himself up. I'd have had no problem bringing him in here the way I'd found him, but I have to admit, there was one hot man lurking under all his scruff and shame. He looks younger, too. Probably in his mid-thirties or so, since he's got some gray and a few lines.

I wonder what he was like before everything went south. The few flickers of a smile I've seen make me think he could light up a room when he's not so depressed. He was probably the life of the party back before—

My jaw drops. *Now* I recognize him.

It has to have been almost two weeks ago. He'd been in a suit just like the one he'd worn earlier tonight. In fact, I think it *was* the same one. Normally I get kind of annoyed with drunk players, since they tend to lose track of what's going on and slow the game down, but he was a happy drunk who could hold his liquor and play cards. All the chairs at my blackjack table had been filled, and he'd managed to get everyone—even the grumpy-ass guy on the end—to join in with some rowdy bantering and trash-talking. It was probably one of the most fun nights I've ever had at the casino. I distinctly remember being disappointed when it was time to bow out and let another dealer take over.

He was a high roller, too. Two hundred dollars per hand, unless he was feeling frisky and upped it to three hundred. After a particularly good run, he'd tipped me two-fifty, and now I actually felt guilty for it. Those chips he'd tossed at me with a wink had been pocket change for him then. They could probably make a world of difference to him now.

Max comes back a moment later with a steaming bowl of soup and carefully sets it down before he sits. Some sort of vegetable mix, judging by the smell and a few pieces of green beans and celery poking through the opaque orange surface.

As he crushes a handful of crackers and sprinkles them into the soup, I clear my throat. "I, um, I think we've met before."

He glances at me, dusting the remaining crumbs off his hands and letting them fall on top of the rest. "Have we?"

"Yeah. I think you played at my table."

His brow furrows. "You said you deal... Blackjack?"

I nod.

He studies me a moment longer, then cracks a faint smile. "Oh yeah. I thought you looked familiar."

I smile back.

He spoons out some soup and blows on it gently. "So how do you like that gig? Dealing cards, I mean?"

"I like it. It has its downsides like any jobs, and there are days when I want to strangle the pit boss, but..." I shrug. "It pays enough for my lifestyle. And it's fun."

He tests the soup gingerly, and apparently decides it's cool enough. After he's eaten a few spoonfuls, he meets my gaze. "What about your other job?"

I try not to bristle. His initial reaction to finding out I'm a stripper surprised me—most people wrinkle their nose or get a little uncomfortable. For Max, it was just a confirmation of something he'd already figured out, and the part where I take off my clothes didn't seem to bother him.

"I like it too," I say. "It also has its moments, and I also want to choke my boss sometimes, but it's not bad."

"You don't have problems with customers being grabby or anything like that?"

"Sometimes. But that's why we have bouncers there who are five times my size. I probably deal with just as many assholes there as I do at the card table."

"Do the ones at the card table try to put their hands on you, though?"

"Nah." I pause for a sip of my water. "Not with the men, anyway. But if they fuck with the female dealers or with the dancers?" I shake my head. "Security takes care of it."

"The dance—oh, right. Your casino is the one with the strippers by the card tables."

"The one?" I chuckle. "A lot of places do that now."

"So I noticed," he said, and spoons out some more soup.

I'm actually a bit surprised that he did notice. Not just because he was drunk and might be a little foggy about that night anyway, but at the time, he just…didn't seem to notice. My casino's got small platforms where topless dancers get up and shake their butts and boobs. The dealers don't see it—our backs are to them—but they're in plain view of the players. Which is the idea. It's hard to count cards when there's tits and ass on display.

I always know when the dancers go up because the music gets loud and the lights start flashing. I've even been known to split my tips with one if she makes a point of really working it to distract the hell out of someone who's counting cards at my table.

Max didn't give the dancers a second look. He glanced at them a time or two, but not with a whole lot of interest. More like, "*Oh. Someone's dancing. Okay.*" And then back to his cards.

I try not to squirm in my seat, remembering how badly I'd wanted to work up the nerve to offer to meet him in the bar. But he was a high roller. Way out of my league. And just because he wasn't into the topless dancers didn't *necessarily* mean he was gay.

He glances up from scraping the remnants of his soup from the bottom of the bowl. "You cold?"

"Hmm?" Oh. Apparently I did squirm. "No. No, I'm good."

He doesn't push the issue. After a moment, he sets the bowl aside and smiles. "I feel so much better. Thank you again. You really, really didn't have to do this."

I return the smile. "Don't mention it."

His expression falters a bit, and he avoids my gaze. Some color blooms in his cheeks. "So, um. You said there's a shelter near here."

"Yeah. I don't know how much space they have or… anything, really. But it's got to be better than sleeping on the streets."

"Most things are better than that." He scrubs a hand over his face, and he suddenly looks really tired. Which reminds me I'm tired. My feet still hurt and my body still aches, and my head's starting to throb a bit in that way it does when I've been awake too long.

"Listen, um…" I drum my fingers on the table. "Not asking for details, or to pry, but…where will you go after this?"

He sighs, deflating. "I don't know. I really don't."

"Where was home before you came here?"

Max swallows. "Doesn't really matter. It's gone."

My chest aches. I can't even imagine. "Well…"

He studies me.

I shift in my seat and absently run a finger around the rim of my empty water glass. "Maybe I can help."

His eyebrows shoot up. Then he quickly shakes his head. "You've already done way too much. I'm a stranger, remember?"

"Yeah, but…"

A memory flickers through my mind of him winking as he tossed me two hundreds and a fifty.

I take a breath. "When you were at my table, you tipped me two hundred and fifty." He winces like I've just kicked him the balls, so I quickly add, "That's more than enough to get you a bus ticket to… well, somewhere."

Max searches my eyes.

"Probably a motel room or something too." I fight the urge to squirm under his scrutiny. "Or…you could… You could stay with me. For a couple of nights."

He straightens, lips parting. "I couldn't ask you to put me up."

"You're not. I'm offering." And every instinct should be telling me this is a terrible idea. A dangerous one. Max seems harmless, but he could be a con artist or an ax murderer or something. But somehow… I don't think he is. I've always been guarded around people, and I've always assumed the worst about their intentions. For some reason I can't explain, Max doesn't ping my prickly defensive exterior.

"Why are you so generous with me?" His whisper barely carries across the table.

"Because you're someone I can help."

"But why do you want to?"

"Does it matter?"

He holds my gaze. After a moment, he lets his drop, and he sighs. "I really don't know what to say. Just bringing me here"—he motions at our surroundings—"is more than I would have asked of someone I know, never mind a stranger."

I'm not sure how to convince him, so I go on like he's already agreed to it. "My house is only about twenty minutes from here. Well, I mean, we're still about a fifteen-minute walk from my car, but if we leave now, we'll be at the house in like half an hour."

Another long silence while we have an awkward staring contest.

Then his shoulders sag, and he says, "Thank you. I'm... God, I'm completely blown away by this. I can't even tell you."

"Don't mention it." I nod past him. "You want to grab anything else before we go?" I'm fucking exhausted and can't wait to faceplant in a pillow, but I'd feel guilty prying a starving man out of a restaurant.

He glances back and considers it for a moment but shakes his head. "No. I think this is enough for me for now."

"Okay. Let's go."

~*~

I'm always a little uncertain when I bring someone to my house. Doesn't even matter that tonight's guest has been sleeping on concrete and park benches for the past week. He's also got on shoes that probably cost as much as my car, and even if his past life really was a "gilded cage on top of an ivory tower built on sand," he's obviously tasted the finer things in life.

So even though my house is the alternative to a crappy hotel or a homeless shelter, I cringe a bit as I pull through the entrance to the trailer park.

It's not one of those rundown shitholes like you see on TV. The ones where they portray everyone in a mobile home as being inbred, toothless, beer-drinking degenerates. Most of the people here are either retired or single moms. The homes are well kept, and even though I do loathe the odd Astroturf lawn, most of the yards are pretty nice too. Me, I've got a little plastic picket fence that the previous owners put up, and inside that, a rock garden with some cactus at the foot of Pablo, the old plastic flamingo I repainted to look like a buzzard.

I pull into the carport and cautiously glance at Max, wondering what he thinks of all this. Has he ever even set foot in a trailer park?

He probably doesn't think much of anything at the moment—he's sound asleep in the passenger seat.

I turn off the engine and give him a gentle nudge. "Hey. We're here."

He jumps, yawns, and looks around. "Damn. Didn't realize I'd dozed off on you."

"Don't worry about it."

We get out, and I'm not sure he even notices our surroundings as he follows me inside.

"So, like I said, it isn't much. I can show you—hang on, gotta take care of this." I drop my keys on the counter next to the coffeepot and the fish tank. I quickly open the plastic fish food canister, tap some into the water, and make sure all three fish are coming out of their rocks to eat. Once they're all accounted for, I close the tank and the food. "Anyway. I'll show you around."

I lead him from the kitchen into the living room. "Bedroom is down that way." I gesture at the hallway. "The master bathroom's in there, and there's another at the other end of the house." I motion over my shoulder.

Max nods slowly. "Great. This is perfect." He sets his bag at his feet and rolls his shoulders, sighing heavily. "I am insanely grateful. You don't even know."

"It's fine." I pause. "You're welcome to take my bed tonight if you want. I can sleep on the couch."

"No, no." He shakes his head. "I'm not kicking you out of your bed after everything you've done for me."

"Max, you're taller than I am, and I can barely sleep on that thing." I nod toward the bedroom. "You'd be much more comfortable in there."

"I'd rather not. I can make do on the couch—trust me."

"It's your call."

"Couch, then." He pauses. "Do you mind if I grab a shower, though?"

"Not at all. It's in the master bathroom."

# Chapter 4
## Max

I thought shaving and brushing my teeth felt good. Turns out it has nothing on a hot shower, especially after I'm already feeling good from having had a decent meal for once. By the time I turn off the water and start drying off with one of Adrian's gigantic and super plush bath towels, I'm so relaxed I can barely stay on my feet. I just try not to think about tomorrow or any point in the future beyond going to sleep. After all, this is a temporary fix. Everything beyond tonight is a big void of *I have no fucking idea*.

Tonight, I'll sleep. I'll enjoy every single minute of sleep on a surface that's not made out of wood or concrete. Whatever comes next, I'll deal with it when it happens.

I dry off, brush my teeth again, and pull my jeans back on. At least they're clean enough to sleep in.

When I return to the living room, Adrian is on his phone again, but he lowers it as soon as I come in the room. Probably just passing the time until he has his bathroom and bedroom back. Considering he was heading home from work when he found me, and that was a couple of hours ago, he must be wiped out.

He gestures at the couch. "I found a couple of pillows and a set of sheets and blanket. It probably won't get too cold in here tonight, but if it does, there's more in the linen closet, which is right outside the smaller bathroom."

"This is perfect. Thank you."

He smiles, and the fatigue is really showing now. "I guess I'll see you in the morning?"

"Yeah. See you in the morning."

He goes into the bedroom, turning off the hall light behind him, and the bedroom door quietly clicks shut. For the first time since he stopped beside me on the sidewalk, I'm alone.

It feels okay, though. As I arrange the blankets and pillows, and figure out a way to lie on the couch without wrenching my back or crunching my neck, I don't feel particularly...lonely. Or at least, no more than I did in the weeks leading up to everything going to shit. Adrian is a complete stranger, and he's in another room, but his presence is more than I've had in a lot longer than I care to think about right now. After this much soul-crushing solitude, I'll take what I can get.

Adrian's right about the couch. I'm six foot exactly, and even with my head on one armrest, my feet are on the other. There's a hard spot in the middle that my hip can't seem to avoid, and it's narrow enough that I'm afraid I'll tumble onto the floor if I try to roll over.

It's also the most comfortable thing I've ever tried to sleep on.

And in no time flat, I'm out cold.

~*~

Adrian has some sheer blue curtains over his windows, and they mercifully filter out some of the brutal desert sunlight. As I sit up slowly, kneading a crick out of my neck, the room is still painfully bright, but it's bearable.

I swing my legs off the couch and stretch. The house is silent except for the filter on the fish tank and the low hum of the refrigerator. Adrian's bedroom door is still closed, so I'm guessing he's still asleep.

As I rub a knot out of my back, I survey my surroundings for the first time. I was dead on my feet when we came in last night—this morning?—and don't remember much besides that amazing shower. Now that I'm a bit more coherent, I look around.

Adrian's living room is sparsely but tastefully decorated. Not quite minimalist, but no more than one person really needs. There's a modest flat screen attached to the wood-paneled wall, surrounded by a handful of photos of people I assume are his family. The simple black coffee table has a small stack of magazines—some devoted to photography, others about geocaching, and some familiar news magazines—and a neat row of remote controls beside a stack of coasters.

On the end table by my pillow, there's a framed photo from a wedding. I pick it up and bring it closer so I can see the faces. The men are all definitely related. I actually have to really look before I figure out that the best man is Adrian and the groom is—I assume—his brother.

I'm envious as I look at each smiling face in turn. No one seems to be pretending to be genuinely happy. Or pretending to like each other.

Sighing, I put the picture back on the table, then stand and work another crick out of my back. There's definitely going to be a bruise on my hip where that hard thing in the couch had been digging in. Still—best sleep I've had in ages.

Slowly, reality dawns on me. It really was the best sleep I've had in ages. Like… years. Thinking back, I honestly can't remember a night when I slept like that. No tossing and turning and stressing over work. No listening to the emptiness of my condo and realizing how painfully alone I was. No passing out when my liver had finally had enough or when even the hard concrete and cold desert night couldn't keep me awake anymore.

*How long have I been this fucked up?*

I can't put a number on it, so I settle on the closest answer: too long. I just hope to God there's still a way to unfuck my life.

The kitchen door opens, startling me, and I turn as Adrian walks into the living room. Instead of black jeans and that tight shirt, he's in a white tank top and red running shorts now. He takes out his earbuds and peels off the iPhone strapped to his sculpted upper arm.

"Hey." He smiles. "How'd you sleep?"

"Better than I have in years." He probably thinks I'm exaggerating. I don't try to change his mind.

"I'm just going to grab a shower." He toes off his running shoes and nudges them up against the wall into the neat row with his sneakers and a pair of black boots. "There's coffee if you want some."

Coffee. Oh God yes.

"Sure. Thanks."

While he's taking his shower, I go into the small kitchen. There are a couple of ceramic mugs hanging above the coffee maker, so I pluck one down and fill it. Normally I like some milk and sugar in my coffee, but I feel weird rifling through his fridge or cabinets, so I drink it black. Which is fine. It's good coffee, so it's not half bad even like this.

There's a fish tank on the counter, which I vaguely remember from last night when he stopped to feed the inhabitants. Careful not to spill my coffee, I lean down to look inside. It's one of those small tanks, kind of like a kid would use as a terrarium for a pet hamster or something. The bottom is an inch deep or so with fluorescent blue rocks, and a few plants stick up on either side of a garish purple castle. Behind another cluster of plants, a filter bubbles quietly.

I can't see any fish at first, but then realize there's one in the window of the castle. A moment later, another cuts a lazy path across the bottom of the tank. They're bright blue, but I know nothing about fish so I wouldn't know what to call them. If he had goldfish or Siamese fighting fish, maybe. Beyond that, my knowledge of fish starts and ends with what's on a sushi menu.

The sound of bare feet on linoleum turns my head, and I very nearly fumble my coffee. Adrian's hair is wet, smoothed out of his face, and he's down to a pair of black shorts and nothing else.

*Whoa.*

He doesn't quite have a six-pack, but he looks like he's only a few intense workouts away from one. He's slim and smooth all over, with a hint of dark hair on his chest and a more pronounced line extending downward from his navel. Just above his right hip is a dragon tattoo, its tail hidden by his low slung waistband.

I gulp and turn back to the fish before I start getting a hard-on. This guy picked me up off the street—no need to test his goodwill by openly perving on him.

"So, you like fish?" It's a stupid question, but marginally better than anything else I might say if I spend another second looking at him.

"Eh, the place felt a little empty without any other living things in it, and I'm better at keeping fish alive than houseplants." He pours himself a cup of coffee, oblivious to the drop of water sliding off his hair and onto his slender shoulder. "I'm not home enough for a dog, and I'm deathly allergic to cats, so..." He nods toward the fish, which causes a few more drops to sprinkle onto his back. "Fish."

I laugh. "I never thought of fish as providing much company."

Adrian shrugs and leans against the counter, cradling his coffee in both hands. "You live alone, you find all kinds of ways to fill in the silence."

My humor fades. I shift my attention back to the fish.

"Oh." Adrian clears his throat. "I'm sorry. That might've been…"

"It's all right." I take a sip of my cooling black coffee. "It isn't like I've told you more than one or two things about me, so I can't expect you to know where all the landmines are."

He says nothing, and just drinks his coffee. His is black too. After a long moment of silence, he meets my gaze. "I won't lie—I'm curious. About you. About how you ended up where you are. But you don't have to tell me anything. If it's none of my business, it's none of my business."

My first instinct is to take him up on that and never say another word about anything that happened before last night. At the same time, though, I want to. Not because I owe him an explanation—I owe him a hell of a lot more than that—but because I'm starting to think it'll eat me alive if I'm the only one who knows.

I take a swallow of coffee and set the cup in front of the fish tank. "The short version is that I am a walking cliché. I came to Las Vegas to…" The words stick in my throat. I'd never said them out loud, and I can't now, so I settle on, "Go out with a bang, I guess."

His thin eyebrows lift. "You were going to kill yourself."

My coffee threatens to come back up. I can't say it, but he sure can. Staring at the pastel yellow and white linoleum at our feet, I go on. "In the last year and a half, I've basically lost everything. My job. My house. My boyfriend."

I steal a glance at him, curious if he reacts to the mention of a boyfriend. If it even registers, I can't see it.

I clear my throat. "There was… It's a long story. A lot of bullshit. In a nutshell, my job was my life. Eighty hours a week for sixteen years. The only reason I even had a boyfriend was we met at a conference, and after three years, he got tired of being my mistress while I was married to my job. So he left. Then I had some health problems. Mostly from burnout. Needed some time off to recover, and the firm decided they could do without me."

Adrian does respond to that, standing a little straighter and cocking his head. "That's illegal, isn't it?"

"Only if they tell you it's why they're firing you."

He rolls his eyes. "Guess that happens in every field."

"Oh yeah. Problem is, I'd advanced enough in my career to command a decent salary… for a job that kids coming out of college will gladly do for a fraction of the price." I pause. "Not that I blame them. I mean, they're coming out of school so far in debt they'll probably pass it on to their grandkids. But it put me in this really shitty position where no one would hire me for what I was qualified to do because they didn't want to pay me, but I was overqualified for everything else."

Adrian whistles. "Jesus."

"And when you live and breathe your job, and it's suddenly gone…" I swallow, an all too familiar lump rising in my throat. "What's left, you know?"

"I can't imagine."

"After the condo was foreclosed, I just…" I keep staring at the floor. "I lost it, I guess. I had a decent amount in savings, but couldn't get a loan without a job. Couldn't even rent an apartment. My career was over, my house and car were gone, the man I loved was gone… I had nothing." I push out a ragged breath and look at Adrian. "I was so depressed, I finally just decided to take the money I had left, come to Vegas, blow every last penny, and then…" I shift uncomfortably. "Be done with it."

I'm not sure what kind of reaction I expect. At this point, I'm mostly concerned about keeping my coffee down, but I'm also curious how he'll respond to this. How stupid it must sound.

He watches me for a moment, then quietly asks, "What changed your mind?"

"About ending it?"

Adrian nods. There's another teardrop of water sliding from his hair, this time along the curve of his throat and down toward his collarbone. I want to watch it, but I don't want to stare.

I rest my hands on the edge of the counter. "It probably sounds insane."

"You're still alive, so it can't be that insane."

He has a point.

"Well." I drum my fingers rapidly. "I was sitting there looking at the painkillers I planned to use, and just thought, that's it? I've been working my ass off my whole life, and now I'm going to be some pathetic body that the hotel maid finds?" I shake my head and shudder at the memory. "And I realized… I mean, this is rock bottom. This is as low as it gets. I literally have nothing. But I don't want to die like that. I don't…" I hesitate, not sure how to word it. "I don't want my life to mean nothing just because the company I worked for decided I do. And I figured, if I could just hold on and not go through with it, maybe I could find some way to get back on my feet. Or die trying." I laugh, sounding both sad and bitter. "At least then I wouldn't be giving up, you know?"

"Wow," Adrian breathes. "That's…a close fucking call."

*You don't know the half of it.*

I don't say it, though. He doesn't need to know just how far I'd pulled the trigger before coming to my senses. So I just mutter, "No kidding."

"How long were you out there on the street? After you…changed your mind?"

I shrug. "A week or so. I kind of lost track of the days. And honestly? I'm not sure how much longer I would've lasted. So I'm, uh, really glad you found me when you did."

"Yeah." He holds my gaze. "Me too."

L.A. WITT

# Chapter 5
## Adrian

Max's story rattles me right to the core. I've been through some low periods in my life, and some of those *just* tickled the edges of the darkness where suicide becomes an option. The darkness has never closed in far enough to make me sit down with a bottle of pills, though, let alone after one last hurrah to blow the last of my money.

I barely know him, but the thought of how close he came... It shakes something in me. He could've so easily been just another body found by another hotel maid. Those make the news sometimes if nothing else is going on, and even then they usually get tucked into a corner of the paper around page seven, between the road construction updates and clearance sale ads for a local sporting goods store. Chances are, if he'd gone through with it, his name wouldn't have even been mentioned, and he'd have faded into the dust like so many people who come to this place to end it. I never would have known that the happy-go-lucky guy who'd tipped me two-fifty after livening up my table for a few hours had died. That when he'd been giving us all the night of our lives just by being there, he'd really been inching toward a ledge.

But he didn't go through with it, and now he's here in my kitchen, drinking coffee and watching my fish.

I swallow some of my own coffee. "So what are you going to do now?"

He gazes at the fish, and slowly shakes his head. "I have no idea. I honestly hadn't thought past getting out of bed this morning."

I gnaw my lip. "Well, we could start with breakfast. I make a damn good omelet."

When he faces me, he has that same look he gave me when we met on the sidewalk. A little bit wary and a little bit curious. "I don't want to keep taking advantage of you."

*You can take advantage of—*

I shove that thought aside before it makes me blush. "Actually you'd be helping me. These eggs will go bad if I don't use them."

His lips quirk a little. I'm not sure if he believes me, but he doesn't seem to have much fight in him. Just telling that story seems like it took a lot out of him. "Sure. An omelet sounds great." He pauses. "And don't let me leave without some way to contact you. I *will* make this up to you once I'm on my feet."

I just give him a little smile, then start rooting around in the fridge to find everything I need. Turns out I still have some ham and cheese too, and the onions haven't wilted after all, so it's Denver omelets today.

As I nudge everything around the skillet with a spatula, he pours himself some more coffee.

"Listen," I say. "I have to work tonight. Need to take off around four." I glance at him. "You're welcome to stay here again if you want to."

"Are you sure?"

"Totally." I nod toward the portable phone on the counter. "If you need to make any calls, that's a Vonage phone. Doesn't cost me a thing no matter where you're calling."

He eyes the phone, and something in him visibly relaxes. "Oh. Okay. Yeah, I... I might make some calls back home. See if anyone can help me find some kind of work."

I turn the omelet, and as the cheese sizzles, glance at him again. "Where is back home, anyway?"

Without looking at me, he quietly says, "L.A. Not that I can afford to live there again unless I hit the lottery, but maybe some of my connections are worth trying." He pauses. "That, and I have a storage unit out there. Paid up through the end of the year. I might as well see about selling all that shit so I at least have some cash to work with, because right now?" He laughs into his coffee cup. "I've got about twelve bucks to my name."

The mention of the storage unit is a relief. At least that gives him something to work with, even if it's just stuff he can pawn for a few hundred dollars.

"If there's anything I can do to help—"

"No." He shakes his head. "You've already done enough. Just letting me crash here and use your phone is huge."

We lock eyes and both smile.

The omelet is done, so I carefully slide it onto a plate. I dig a fork out of a drawer and hand everything to him. "There's ketchup and tabasco in the fridge if you want it."

"No, this is fine." He balances his plate on his forearm and slices off a piece of egg with the fork. "Thanks."

"Any time." I crack an egg to get my own breakfast going. "You need anything from town before I leave for work? We're, uh, not exactly walking distance from anything except a 7-11. And you can help yourself to what's in the fridge. I haven't been shopping this week, but I doubt anything's expired."

"I'll be fine. Just tell me how to get to the 7-11. I've got enough cash to get something there to tide me over for the evening." He pauses. "Do you by chance have a washing machine?"

43

"Yeah. As soon as we're done here, I'll show you how to use it. The dryer is a little temperamental, but it gets the job done."

"Sounds perfect."

~*~

My brain is numb and my wrists are getting tired when my relief shows up. I thank the players, all of whom have been sitting there for at least an hour, and bow out while Jamie steps in to take my place.

"Hey. West." Kelly, the pit boss, nudges my arm. "Can I borrow you for a second?"

I'm itching to go get something to eat, but don't let my irritation show. "What's up?"

She moves in a little closer and drops her voice so only I can hear. "You doing okay today?"

"Yeah, sure. Why?"

"Don't know. You've just seemed a bit preoccupied since you got here."

I hesitate, but we've known each other for years, and Kelly's good people. "I, um…" I glance around.

"You know what? Let's do this somewhere else." She cranes her neck and looks past me. With a gesture toward the office, she lets the other pit boss know she's stepping out. Apparently there's no objection, and we're on our way off the casino floor.

In the back office, she drops into a chair and gingerly rubs her ankle. I do the same. As we both knead our tender feet, she says, "So what's going on?"

"Well." I gulp. "So I…might've taken in a homeless dude last night."

Her hands freeze and her eyes are suddenly huge. "Come again?"

My face burns. I stare down, focusing on massaging the fatigue out of my left foot. "I can't explain it. I was walking back to my car after my shift at the NightOwl, and... I don't know. I just couldn't walk by him."

She sits back, her sore feet apparently forgotten. "So what happened?"

"I bought him dinner. And I was going to drop him at the homeless shelter, but I ended up letting him crash at my place instead."

"My God, Adrian." She clicks her tongue. "It's one thing when you pick up questionable pieces of ass. Taking a bum home is a whole different thing."

"He's not..." I sigh. "He's not just some bum. The guy hit some bad luck, and—"

"And just needs someone to take him in and help him until he gets back on his feet." She rolls her eyes. "How have you been a dealer this long without knowing a con artist when you see one?"

"Except he's dug his heels in every time I've offered something. I've had to talk him into everything. Even breakfast."

"Well yeah. He doesn't want to seem too desperate or you'll catch on."

Huh. Okay. She... She kind of does have a point.

I move to my right foot and focus on that. "The thing is, I've seen him before. He actually played at my table. Before he ended up on the street, I mean."

"So he's a gambling addict?" she sputters. "Honey, he's—"

"No! No. He came to Vegas to..." I trail off, already anticipating her response, and now that I hear it in my head, I realize what a gullible idiot I am. Oh fuck, he's probably robbing me blind while I'm here at work, convinced I helped someone in need. No good deed goes unpunished, right? "Aw, crap."

"Oh my God, honey." She covers her face with her hands and groans. Then she drops them into her lap. "You know you just got conned, right?"

I'm queasy all of a sudden. There is literally nothing I can say to reassure her that Max isn't like that. Because he's a stranger. And if he really is a con artist, I can't take a single word that came from his mouth at face value.

But if he were a con artist, why would he be out on the street in an expensive suit and shoes? Because then he'd look even more like someone respectable who lost his shirt.

But if he were playing me, why didn't he have a more elaborate tearjerker of a story to tug at my heartstrings? Because apparently he didn't need one.

But nobody can fake that kind of shame, sadness, and desperation, right? Uh, just because they're not doing it in front of a camera and hoping to win an Oscar…

I swear under my breath. Wow. I've never thought of myself as a gullible idiot, but here I fucking am.

"Where is he now?" Her tone is laced with suspicion. When I don't answer immediately, she says, "*Adrian?*"

"Um…"

"Oh for fuck's sake." She stands, groaning and wincing. "Honey, why don't you take the rest of the night off. I think you need to go de-bum your place before he relieves you of anything valuable."

I wince, but I can't really argue. Fuck. Since when am I this stupid?

"Okay. I'll, uh, go clock out."

~*~

My hands are shaking as I open the storm door, and I almost drop my keys when I go to unlock the main door. In my mind, I can see my house ransacked, everything I own destroyed or stolen. He'd at least leave the fish alone, right?

The lock gives, and I push open the door so hard I stumble into the house.

Max is sitting on the couch, and jumps. "Oh. Hey. I thought you were working late tonight."

"I, um..." I look around. As near as I can tell, nothing has moved. My leather jacket is still hanging on the coat hook. The fish are still happily swimming in their tank. The old pickle jar that's three-quarters full of change is still sitting on top of the fridge, a box of crackers leaning precariously against it just like I'd left it this morning. "I got off early."

"Oh."

I drop my keys and gaming license on the counter and pause to feed the fish. Then I go into the living room. He's got a spiral notebook in front of him with some notes—names and phone numbers, by the looks of it—and a pack of red licorice. The handset for my Vonage phone is sitting beside the notebook.

"So what are you up to?" I ask.

He shrugs. "Made a few calls. Nobody's making any promises at this point, but it's a place to start."

"Oh. Good. Good to hear. That's..." I'm not sure what to say, but I seriously feel like an asshole. Kelly was right that taking in a random stranger was incredibly stupid. If I'd come back here and found the place ransacked, I'd have deserved it. But did I really think that was Max?

"Hey." He draws me out of my thoughts. "Something wrong?" His brow is pinched, and I can feel his apprehension from here. Like he's bracing himself for me to tell him he's overstayed his welcome and would he please show his sorry ass to the homeless shelter. Because I don't already feel like a gigantic bag of dicks.

Sighing, I sink onto the couch beside him, but don't look at him. "I...told one of my coworkers about this. About taking you in. And she got me all worked up and paranoid that you're a con artist, and she basically sent me home to make sure you hadn't robbed me blind." I covered my face with my hands. "I was actually buying that right up until I got home and realized you're just…" I motion toward his notes and the phone.

"Well, she's partly right."

My head snaps toward him.

A smirk plays at his lips, and he holds up the pen he's been using. "I did steal this from you."

I stare at him incredulously, then laugh. "You're a dork."

He chuckles. "I also did a small load of laundry and swiped a Coke from the fridge." He holds out his hands, wrists together. "So, if you want to cuff me and place me under citizen's arrest… I'll understand."

Our eyes lock, and we both burst out laughing.

I sigh and shift my attention to the coffee table to avoid his gaze. "I'm sorry. I…feel like an ass for thinking the worst of you."

"I can't really blame you. You don't know me from Adam." He pauses. "I was a little nervous about taking you up on your offer, to be honest."

I turn to him again. "Really?"

Max nods. "I don't know you. How could I know what your motives really were?"

I swallow. It hadn't even occurred to me that he might think I was the shady one. Looking him up and down, I say, "I think you've got the physical advantage."

"Not when I've eaten the equivalent of one tiny meal over the course of a week."

"Oh."

"And if you'd had some kind of weapon or something…" He shrugs. "So I was nervous, and I could tell you were too. I'm not insulted by it."

"Well, that's a relief." Exhaling slowly, I lean back against the couch. "I guess this means we were both stupid to some extent."

Max leans back too, and slings his arm across the cushion between us. "Risks are part of life. I'm just really glad we both took this one."

I meet his gaze and smile. "Yeah. Me too."

It's weird—all the way here, I was convinced I was going to come in and find I'd been robbed. Now that I'm sitting here looking at him, that thought seems absurd. I barely know him. It's been less than twenty-four hours since I couldn't walk away from him by the Bellagio fountain. But in some way I can't explain, I feel like he's been here all along. Like I've known him forever, and expecting him to rob me while I was at work makes about as much sense as expecting Mrs. Hawthorne, the sweet old lady next door, to do it.

I break eye contact and clear my throat. "Well, since I'm home—are you hungry?"

Max gives a quiet, self-conscious chuckle. "I think I'm going to be in a constant state of 'I could eat' for a while." He pauses. "But I don't want to eat you out of house and home or—"

"Don't worry about it. You like pizza?"

"Who doesn't?"

"My younger sister, but she's strange." I wave a hand and get up. "Want me to order something?"

Max sighs, and I already know that sigh well. "Adrian, I—"

"Chill. I've got a two-for-one coupon for a place that delivers here. So yours would be free anyway. And they're big enough we'll have leftovers for breakfast. If, uh, you're good with pizza for breakfast."

He studies me like he's completely baffled by my offer. "I'm... Yeah, I like pizza for breakfast." Another self-conscious laugh. "It'll be just like my college days."

"Perfect." I take out my cell phone. "Let me get the coupon off the fridge and order."

# Chapter 6
## Max

I'm sure that a few months ago, I'd have turned up my nose at this kind of pizza. If it didn't come from an authentic Italian place—the kind that does a proper thin crust and uses an actual homemade sauce—then forget it. All the "30 minutes or less" chains? No, thank you.

Tonight, one bite of this thick, greasy pizza, and I'm in heaven. The cheese probably came pre-grated, the dough was probably pre-formed and frozen, and the sauce probably came out of a tub—not even a jar, but a *tub*— and it's the most delicious thing I've ever eaten. Amazing what a week of barely eating does to one's palate.

We're at Adrian's dining room table since he felt weird about eating where I sleep. The pizza box is propped up against some magazines and mail stacked at one end of the table, and the other is already in the fridge. It's funny how alien it is, the idea of knowing there's food for tomorrow. Breakfast, hell—there's no way we'll finish this pizza, and the other will probably cover breakfast *and* lunch.

Assuming I'm still here. As kind as he's been, I'm still expecting the other shoe to drop at any moment. I doubt he's gone into this thinking I'll be having mail delivered to his couch. Fortunately, I made a little progress getting my shit together today, and if he's serious about letting me stay until breakfast, I'll be in good shape.

After two slices of pizza, I sit back and sip my Coke. "So, um. I got in touch with an old colleague. He's going to wire me some money in the morning."

"Oh. Good." Adrian dabs a paper napkin at a spot of sauce on the corner of his mouth.

"It'll be enough for a bus ticket back to L.A., and then some. Once I'm there, he says he'll put me up for a few days until I can find a place." My heart sinks a bit at the thought. "Not that I'll be able to find one for a while, but…it's something." A foreclosure and a repo on my credit report, along with being unemployed for the better part of a year and having precisely nothing for first and last month's rent—oh yeah, I'm a landlord's *dream*. "Anyway, I'll figure it out. I… Do you mind if I crash here one more night? I'll be out of your hair tomorrow, as soon as he wires—"

"Of course." Adrian sips his soda. "I'm not going to throw you out."

"Which I appreciate, but I really don't want to take advantage of you."

"It's fine. Really." He pauses. "I'm not sure where to pick up a wire transfer here, but we can just google Western Union locations, I guess. Once he tells you it's gone through, I can drive you there and then to the bus station."

Every time he casually tells me he's going to do one more thing to help me, it blows my mind. I had to sift through dozens of acquaintances, colleagues, distant relatives, and people who I guess are friends before I found someone I could even think to call for help. Dozens more before I found one who said he would.

And yet this complete stranger…

My mouth has gone dry, so I take another swallow of Coke. "You want to hear something crazy? Or, well, pathetic?"

Adrian's eyebrows lift. *Okay?*

"If I were able to get on Facebook right now, I've probably got... I don't know, a thousand friends? Mostly old colleagues and people I went to school with. Today, I spent an hour jotting down names of people I knew and might be able to reach by phone who *might* help me. That first list? Probably two pages long. The second?" I sigh, staring at the grease outline where my last slice of pizza had been on my plate. "Five, ten people?"

"Wow, really?"

"Yeah. And I mean... It's not like I've fucked people over or anything. I don't have, like, people with grudges. I just...don't have people."

Adrian blinks. "None?"

"Well, very few. Just about everyone I had any kind of actual relationship with over the last fifteen years or so were colleagues. And after I lost my job..." I gnaw my lip. "I didn't just lose my paycheck, you know? I lost my entire social circle. Everyone."

"You're not still friends even after you lost your job?" His tone is gentle and curious, not judgmental. "I mean, I left one casino a few years ago, and I still meet up with some of the other dealers sometimes. Went to one of their weddings last summer. You weren't close like that?"

I swallow hard. "I thought I was." It's a struggle, but I meet his gaze. "Turns out I was wrong. Once I wasn't part of the firm anymore, I... It's like I ceased to exist."

Adrian sits back a little, pushing out a breath. "Wow."

I clear my throat. "Fortunately, I do have a guy—the one who's wiring me the money. We worked together for a few years and stayed in touch." I laugh bitterly. "Guess I didn't get the memo about cutting off ex-coworkers, but I'm really glad I didn't."

"Yeah, seriously. I'm glad someone's going to help you out, though. I wish there was more I could do."

"More?" I nearly choke on the word. "My God, I couldn't ask you to do any more. You..." I hesitate, my voice getting a little thick. "I'm not joking—you saved my life."

Adrian smiles, and he puts a hand on my forearm. It's the first time he's touched me since we shook hands on the sidewalk, and the soft contact almost moves me to tears. After a week of people stepping around me and making a point of not touching me, after a day of realizing just how few people I really have to fall back on, this almost-stranger's hand on my arm drives home more than ever how profoundly alone I've been for too long.

I put my hand over the top of his, and squeeze. "Thank you. For everything."

"You're welcome."

We hold each other's gazes for a moment. Then we both withdraw our hands, and the moment's gone. My stomach is still fluttery, though. I glance at the pizza and decide two slices might be enough after all. Especially since this won't go to waste—if I decide I'm hungry later, it'll still be here. And so will I.

"So. Um." I clear my throat before my emotions get the best of me. "I'm curious about you."

Adrian tenses slightly. "What about me?"

"Anything, really." I shrug. "What made you go into your line of work?"

"Stripping?" There's a hint of defensiveness in his tone.

"I was thinking card dealing, but…either or? Like I said, I'm just curious."

He softens slightly. "I didn't want to go into debt by going to college, and I didn't need a degree to deal cards. So I got my gaming license, started at one of the smaller casinos, and eventually got a job on the Strip."

"Is it really that different? Working on the Strip versus elsewhere?"

"Different crowd, mostly. The tourists mostly stick to the Strip, especially the high rollers." He looks at the pizza for a second like he's considering another slice. Finally he takes one, sliding it onto his plate. "I find the crowd a little less depressing, to be honest." He picks off a piece of pepperoni and tosses it in his mouth.

"How so?"

"Some of the smaller casinos attract more locals. With fewer tourists and more locals, you see a lot of the same faces." He licks some grease off his thumb and forefinger. "Which means you start figuring out who's addicted. And that gets kind of heartbreaking after a while."

"I can imagine." I decide I could go for some more pizza myself and pull a slice from the box. "The tourists can probably get pretty depressing too. Especially when they... You know..." I still can't believe I was throwing down hundreds on his table less than two weeks ago.

"No one ever said gambling was pretty," he says dryly. "You get kind of numb to it after a while, but it's still sad."

"I believe it."

We nibble our pizza slices in silence for a minute or so.

"I, uh..." I say finally. "I'm curious—and you can tell me it's none of my business—but how did you get into stripping?"

Surprisingly, he doesn't get defensive. He laughs, cheeks coloring as he licks some more grease off his thumb. "On a dare."

"A dare? Really?"

"Well, technically two dares." He chuckles as he wipes his hands on the napkin. "One of my coworkers and I saw an ad for a pole-dancing class. I dared her to take it, and she dared me to take it with her." He shrugs. "So, I did. And...I liked it. A lot. Enough that we both went back and took the advanced class."

"Decided to go get paid for it?"

"No. I ended up at the NightOwl with her and a few of her friends for a bachelorette party, and she and I started talking shit about how bad the dancers were. After we'd both had a few drinks, she dared me to see if they'd hire me."

I laugh. "Which apparently they did."

"Yeah." He chuckles. "I came back a few nights later, auditioned, and got hired. Never looked back."

"Sounds like you enjoy it."

"I do. And hey, it's motivation to keep myself in shape." He gestures at the pizza. "This is kind of a rare thing for me, but it probably wouldn't be if I didn't have to dance on a pole in booty shorts twice a week."

The image that flickers through my mind is almost unbearably hot, and I have no idea how I keep from shivering. "Damn. I never thought of using that as motivation to keep going to the gym."

"Whatever works, right?"

We both laugh.

He takes a swig of Coke. "There's also the added bonus of occasionally hooking up on the job."

"Oh really?"

He nods, grinning. "I mean, I don't make a habit of it. I'm not a prostitute. Well…not usually."

"What does that mean?"

He watches me for a moment as if he's figuring out how I'll react before he's even spoken. "Sometimes when a guy gets a private dance, he'll offer money to meet him back at his hotel. If it's enough cash to get my attention, and he's sober, attractive, and doesn't peg my psycho radar, it's not below me to take him up on it. Mostly I ask myself if this is someone I'd hook up with if I'd just met him at a bar. If I would…" He shrugs. "Why not?"

"It's not…dangerous?"

"It is to a degree. That's why I'll only meet him at a hotel where I know someone who works security. I'll let them know I'm coming in, they get a cut of what I make, and they make sure there's someone on the same floor in case things go south."

"Has it ever gone bad?"

He shakes his head. "Nah. I mean, once in a while the sex is terrible. And then there was the guy who was on a business trip and went to a gay strip club for the first time. Decided he was going to try sex with a man for the first time too. As soon as I walked into his room, the guy has a total breakdown and freaks out, and the next thing I know, he's on the phone with his wife, admitting he's gay and apologizing…" He waves a hand. "I didn't stick around for the rest. Not that I wanted to ditch him, but I got the feeling a gay prostitute wasn't who he needed for company right then." He sighs. "Poor guy."

"No kidding." I pick up my Coke can, and before I take a sip, add, "You must have some stories."

"A few, yeah." He studies me. "You're not like other people."

I assume he isn't referring to the obvious part about being homeless after a Vegas bender. "How so?"

"When I tell people I strip, the reactions are pretty predictable. Most people are disgusted or at least uncomfortable. Others are turned on by it." He narrows his eyes slightly like he's still trying to read me. "Finding out I occasionally prostitute myself usually makes people see me either as someone who views himself as a worthless piece of meat or someone who *is* a worthless piece of meat. But I'm… not really getting that vibe off you."

"You're not a piece of meat." I look him in the eye. "Obviously you went into your job voluntarily and with both eyes open; you enjoy what you do, and you're not reckless about who you sleep with." I shrug. "I'd be worried if it sounded like you were there against your will, but you certainly don't seem to be. And if you're not ashamed of what you do—and I don't think you should be—then who am I to judge?"

His expression offers nothing. "You'd be amazed how many people think that since I use my body for money, it's something to be ashamed of."

"Oh, I know how people feel about it. But you're talking to a man who was chewed up and spat out by a perfectly legitimate and respectable job, to the point it nearly killed me. And when it did reach that point, they tossed me out like last week's garbage." I hold his gaze. "On paper, I wasn't using my body for money, but my medical file will tell you otherwise."

Adrian swallows.

"Coal miners, athletes, construction workers, soldiers," I continue. "They're all using their bodies to make money too, and it takes a heavy toll. I don't think what you're doing is any less moral just because you're undressed."

He squirms a bit. "Not many people get that."

"Not many people have thought about how much their 'respectable' job is killing them. But anyway, without going into a long diatribe about sex and morality, the short version is that if you're an adult who's doing it of your own free will, and you like what you do, then..." I raise my can in a mock toast. "More power to you."

He holds my gaze in disbelief, but then smiles and clinks his can against mine. "Thanks. It's always good to meet someone who doesn't think I lack self-respect just because I strip and occasionally fuck for money."

I just smile. It's hard to put into words that I can't help but respect him. He makes no apologies for who he is. He's sometimes uneasy about how a person might take the information, but never once has he struck me as being embarrassed or regretful about what he does. It's impossible for me not to respect someone like that.

He's not a piece of meat. He's beautiful. Physically and otherwise. Just judging by the way he walks, he must be stunning when he dances.

There's no way to say it without sounding like a perv. No way to convey it without making him think I want to take advantage of him. No way to tell him I'm genuinely intrigued and curious about him and about what he is without sounding like I'm making a pass at him.

But deep down, I wish I could see him dance.

L.A. WITT

# Chapter 7
## Adrian

It's hard to sleep that night. I could've stayed up until dawn talking to Max. He's so easy to talk to and just be with, especially when I can mention my job at the NightOwl without feeling skeevy.

Of course, I find a way to second guess that too. As I'm lying awake in my silent bedroom, I wonder if he just doesn't find me attractive. Maybe he prefers bigger guys. Hairier ones. Or maybe he prefers the opposite direction—the twinks who make me look like a body builder.

It's stupid to read anything into it. So he's being a decent guy and not trying to get into my pants now that he knows I'm a sometimes-prostitute? Maybe it's because he's broke. Two weeks ago, when he was at my table, he had no way of knowing I'd have absolutely taken him up on it if he'd offered enough money. Hell, who was I kidding? I'd have hooked up with him for free. I still would. He's insanely attractive, and he's so sweet.

I refuse to offer, though. I don't want him to think it's a pity fuck. I don't *do* pity fucks. I don't sleep with anyone who doesn't make my blood pump, regardless of how much money they offer.

Max? God, yeah.

I was attracted to him from the moment he sat down at my table, and again when he came out of that casino bathroom after a shave. When I told him I'm a stripper and he responded with curiosity? When I admitted to occasionally having sex for money? Nothing's changed. He doesn't look at me differently. As near as I can tell, he's completely indifferent to me being a sex worker. The things he said about coal miners and athletes don't feel like lip service.

I close my eyes and exhale. Tomorrow, he'll be gone. On his way back to his own life. When I picked him up yesterday, I could honestly say it never occurred to me that I might miss him when he moved on.

But I'm pretty sure I'm going to.

~*~

We both agreed Antonio's pizza tastes even better the next day. Especially cold. After we'd polished off a few slices and thrown back some coffee, he packs up his few possessions so I can drive him into town to pick up his money.

It's late in the afternoon before he gets confirmation that his friend wired the money. Fine by me—we pass the time talking about whatever, and I'm really enjoying his company. If I didn't have to work tonight, I'd happily stay here for a few more hours.

Eventually, though, his friend does calls the house phone to give Max the tracking number for the wire transfer. We head out, and a quick search on my phone brings us to the supermarket I go to. I'd never noticed the Western Union sign, but there it is.

As Max tucks the cash into his wallet, I swear I can feel the tension leaving his neck and shoulders. He's still got a long and bumpy road ahead of him, but after being down to about twelve dollars—less after he bought the notebook and licorice from the 7-11—I can only imagine the relief he feels at having five hundred dollars on him.

"This will definitely get me to L.A." He blows out a breath as we walk toward the parking lot. "A bus ticket isn't all that much, but I'd have been completely out of money when I got there. This gives me some cushion."

"Good." I smile, doing my best to hide the fact that I'm sad to see him go. "I definitely hope things get better for you."

He glances at me, then halts and pulls out his wallet again. He fishes out some twenties. "Here. For everything you've—"

"No." I put up a hand and shake my head. "Once you're back on your feet, if you really want to pay me back, we'll figure it out then." Lowering my hand, I meet his gaze. "That's all you have right now. I'll be fine."

He watches me, the offer still hovering between us. "I just don't... I mean, I feel like..."

I close his fingers around the money and gently press his hand back to him. "Don't. We're good. I promise."

He regards me silently. "I *will* pay you back at some point."

I nod. "Okay. We'll work it out when we get there. But right now? Don't sweat it." Truth is, I don't care if he ever pays me back for anything, but I know he won't stop digging his heels in unless I leave it open-ended. And since I do, he does—he puts the cash back in his wallet and slips it into the pocket of his jeans.

We keep walking toward the car. As we get in and put on our seatbelts, I ask, "So what do you think you'll end up doing? For a job?" I pause. "In fact, I don't even know what you did before."

He smiles faintly. "I was an advertising executive before. Now..." He sighs and stares out the windshield. "I don't know. Whatever I can get, to be honest."

I drive for a few minutes before I speak again. "Do you miss it? Not working yourself into the ground, but…the job?"

Now it's his turn for a long silence. "I miss the creativity. Working on ad campaigns, things like that. But especially the last few years, after I got promoted to the senior position, it was a lot less creative and a lot more corporate. I don't miss that part at all."

"So you went into it because you're a creative type?"

Max nods, and there's a ghost of a smile on his lips. "I would've gone to art school, but everyone told me I needed to get a *career*. Then I'd be stable and could do all the art I wanted in my spare time." He laughs humorlessly. "Spare time. Yeah right."

"What kind of art did you do?"

"Whatever I could get my hands on. Painting and drawing, mostly. Computer imaging was still relatively new when I was in high school, but I got hooked on that too."

I glance at him, and there's a spark in his eye that I haven't seen before. "So, Photoshop? That kind of thing?"

"Oh, I love Photoshop. I was never very good at photography, but when I could take images and play with them on the screen? Man, I can lose hours doing that shit."

I smile. "Yeah, I love that stuff."

"I saw you're into photography." He pauses but quickly adds, "The magazines on your coffee table."

"I am, yeah."

"Any particular subject?"

"I'm not really partial to anything. Except I don't do a lot of people."

"Really?"

"Yeah. Both my jobs mean having people in my face constantly. I guess when I take the camera out, I want to look at other things." I steal another glance at him.

*I might make an exception, though.*

Gaze fixed on something up ahead, Max nods. "I can understand that. I don't think I'd want to paint the shit I stared at all day at work."

"Right?" I chuckle. "So maybe you could find a design job or something."

"I might. I'll probably also see if I can drum up some freelance work." His enthusiasm fades a little. "Assuming I can get my hands on some equipment."

"Like what?"

"Like a laptop and drawing pad. The one I have in storage is just for travel. Checking e-mail and that kind of shit. I never bothered to get one that supported imaging software or peripherals because I had the absolute top of the line gear issued to me from work. Obviously *that's* all gone."

"Ouch."

"Eh. I'll figure something out. When I get back to L.A. and sell off some of the crap I've got in storage, I should be able to scrape together enough for a passable laptop. That'll at least get me in the door for some freelance gigs."

"Good. Good." I turn down the road that will take us toward the Greyhound station, and my stomach knots. Already? "Maybe your next job won't suck up so much of your time. You could get back into painting and stuff."

"That's what I'm hoping." He smiles, and it seems both tired and genuine. "If anything, I think the last year was a wakeup call. I've been working myself to death and forgot to actually live my life. So I'm looking forward to maybe getting it right this time."

"Well, good luck. I really hope things work out better."

"Thanks. Me too."

Conversation has been easy for us since last night, even after I'd convinced myself I'd been conned and he was going to rob me, but as soon as we pass the next sign for the Greyhound station, neither of us says much. He's probably focused on what comes next. Where he'll go. How he's going to tackle this second chance at his own life.

Me, I'm just trying not to let on that I wish he could stay in Las Vegas.

*I just met you. I still want to know you.*

*You're not even gone, and I already miss you.*

I focus on driving and not my ridiculous thoughts. Obviously it's just been too long since I've socialized with someone who isn't on the same payroll. Or someone I met on a get-laid app. A fun but detached fuck isn't quite the same as a long conversation with someone who's also artistic and actually has two brain cells to rub together.

Apparently this is a sign that I need to get out more and connect with people in ways that don't require condoms and lube.

Pulling into the station, I consider parking, but he's a grown man. He doesn't need someone to walk him through buying a ticket and finding his bus. And anyway, that'll just delay the inevitable.

So, I pull up to the curb, and as the engine idles, I turn to him. "Okay. Here we are."

Max unbuckles his seatbelt, picks up his backpack off the floorboards, and rests it on his lap. "All right. Well…" He extends a hand across the console. "Thank you again."

"You're welcome." Shaking his hand doesn't feel quite right, but we don't know each other well enough for a hug, so I let it be. "Stay in touch?"

"Of course." He winks as he lets go of my hand. "I owe you, remember?"

I laugh, but it's hard. I was hoping for a second there that he wanted to stay in touch for the same reasons I did, not because he wants to settle a debt sometime in the future. But still. It's something.

I jot my e-mail address on the back of a gas receipt and hand it to him. "This is also how you can find me on Facebook. Or search for Adrian West."

"Okay." He glances at the e-mail before sliding the receipt into his wallet. "When I get some sort of electronics up and running, I'll friend you. So if a random guy named Max Reynolds sends you a friend request, it's not just some creeper."

I laugh again, and it still takes some work because it doesn't feel like we should be saying goodbye quite yet. Which is stupid because, hello, we absolutely should be. "I'll keep that in mind. In fact..." I take out my phone and tap the Facebook app. Then I hand it over. "If you can find yourself on there and send the request, it'll be there when you log in."

"Good idea." He does a quick search, hits Add Friend, and hands me back the phone. "There you go. We're good."

"Great. Thanks. I'll look forward to seeing you." I hold up my phone. "On Facebook, I mean."

"Likewise." He reaches for the handle on the door, but pauses like he might say something else. I'm not sure why, but I'm holding my breath.

Then he just flashes another smile, thanks me again, and gets out of the car.

I watch until he disappears inside before I finally drive off. As I do, I glance at my phone, which is dark and sitting on the passenger seat he was occupying. At least we have a Facebook connection. Who knows? Maybe we'll strike up a conversation. Maybe he'll find a reason to come back to Vegas, and he'll be game to see me again.

Or maybe I'm losing my mind.

At this point, that's about as safe a bet as any.

L.A. WITT

# Chapter 8
## Max

The only things standing between me and Los Angeles are a bus and a ticket to get on it. I'm not exactly sure how everything will play out once I get there, but this is the next step, and it needs to happen before anything else does.

So why the hell have I been sitting here for an hour and a half?

I stare up at the reader board with the arrivals and departures. The next bus bound for Los Angeles leaves in forty-five minutes. The one after that probably isn't too much later, but it's not on the board yet.

The longer I stay here in Vegas, the longer it'll be before I get my shit together and pull myself up off rock bottom. There's nothing for me here.

Except...there is.

And he left an hour and a half ago.

Exhaling, I rub my eyes with my thumb and forefinger. I'm an idiot. I know I'm an idiot. I know exactly what I need to do to stop being an idiot. We're connected on social media, so it's not like I'm just riding off into the sunset and we'll never see each other again.

But I'm still sitting here, and I still don't have a ticket, and for the four hundredth time since I got here, I'm seriously considering leaving. Not to Los Angeles. To Adrian. I'd never be able to find his place again to save my life, and he never said which casino he works in. But didn't he say he dances at… What's the name of that place? Night Bird? Night… something…?

No. The NightOwl. It's definitely the NightOwl.

My stomach flutters as I entertain the idea again. He said he was on his way there after he dropped me here. Which means it probably won't be long before he's dancing.

I shake myself to get that thought out of my head. If anything will help me pull myself together and get on that bus, it *won't* be thinking about Adrian dancing.

I absently rest my palm on my wallet. It's reassuring to know I've got some actual cash on me now. And I know damn well I need to guard every cent with my life. Funny how I'm even stingier about it now than yesterday. I still felt a little guilty about splurging on that three-dollar bag of red licorice, but giving in to that tiny temptation for a small luxury had made me feel less hopeless. More like myself. A year ago, I didn't have to worry about money at all. Yesterday, being able to treat myself to something I enjoyed had felt…almost like a redemption. Which is stupid, but there it is.

Now that I have five hundred dollars in my wallet, I feel like I'm in the desert and rationing every drop of water. Ironic since I actually am in the desert and will be until I pony up the twenty bucks or so it'll take to get me back to… Well, okay, Los Angeles is a desert too. But a different one. The ocean is there. As is what little of my old life still exists.

So why am I seriously considering blowing some of this cash on a cab ride to the NightOwl to see if Adrian will let me take him out to dinner as a thank-you? No, I can't afford it—not really, considering I don't know how long this money is going to have to tide me over—but it doesn't feel right *not* to.

I tap my fingers on the edge of my wallet. Thinking back to the car ride here, something doesn't seem quite right. He was edgy, especially as we'd gotten closer to the bus station. Not like he'd been when we'd met on the street and he was being understandably cautious. More like...

Fuck, I don't even know. Every theory I come up with sounds like wishful thinking. He didn't want this to be over. He wanted to come in with me. He was going to suggest I stay another night. Odds are, he was probably just itching for me to get out of the car so he could get back to his regularly scheduled life as someone who *isn't* a complete and total loser, even if he occasionally scrapes them up off the pavement.

I don't know what he was thinking when he dropped me off, but I need to. And...I just need to see him again. And do *something* for him to make up for even a fraction of everything he's done for me.

So I get up, walk out, and go looking for a taxi.

~*~

The NightOwl is a couple of blocks off the strip. Close enough you can see the glow of the huge casinos and even hear some of the noise, but it still seems relatively dark and quiet. In any other city, it probably wouldn't even be open this early, but it's Vegas. They've probably got dancers here at ten in the morning.

A bouncer watches me with not a lot of interest as I approach the door. Adrian wasn't kidding about those guys, either. They're probably five times *my* size.

The cover is eight dollars. I wince a little—it already cost me ten to go like four or five miles from the bus station, and it'll probably cost the same to go back assuming I don't just walk. On the other hand, another eight dollars won't break me any more than I'm already broken.

So I pay, leave my bag at coat check, and walk inside.

It's been a long time since I've been to a strip club, but things haven't changed much. It's dark enough to hide the faces of most of the patrons, with bright, colorful lights over the round stage in the middle and behind the liquor above the bar. The music is loud, and the dancer on the stage right now has the attention of the four or five guys sitting closest to its edge.

I wonder if strippers have to be extra acrobatic in a city where Cirque du Soleil and all those other shows are the norm. That, or this guy just really likes to show how strong and flexible he is, pulling himself up and down the pole and lifting his feet completely off the floor as if it's the easiest thing in the world. If not for the occasional twitch of his lips, it would look effortless.

A bartender is giving me the side-eye. I'm not sure if there's an actual drink minimum here, but apparently I'm expected to get something. He's annoyed when I just order a Coke; I don't bother explaining that I have to conserve money as badly as I do.

As I'm turning back from the bar toward the stage, the song changes. The dancer picks up a few crumpled and folded bills that have accumulated around him and gives a few winks and flirty looks to the men around him. Someone reaches out with some more money in his hand—looks like a couple of hundreds—and the stripper gives a nod toward the opposite side of the room. There, another bouncer stands guard by a doorway. Above that, a red neon sign says *Private Booths*.

The stripper makes a graceful dismount from the stage, takes the man with the hundreds by the hand, and they disappear through the doorway under the sign. I stare at it for a moment, though I'm not really sure why. I'm not even sure why I'm here. Or more to the point, what I expect to happen now that I am.

The music starts again, and when I turn, more men have gathered around the stage, and there's another dancer at its center.

It's him.

It's Adrian.

And my God, he's beautiful.

His hips move like they've got a mind of their own even in those skintight leather shorts. He's got a gorgeous ass, which doesn't surprise me in the least but definitely makes the Coke in my hand seem like it needs to be a lot colder. He's got on a sheer black top, but that's gone before the first verse is over, and I just... I just stare.

It's easy for a strip show to be sleazy. In fact, it's kind of hard not to with a group of men leering and drooling and throwing money. But Adrian struts around that stage like he's got them all wrapped around his finger. Sure, they might think he's a piece of meat, and he might be up there for their entertainment, but when he smirks or winks or slowly licks his lips or undulates dangerously close to a sweaty man's face, he's in charge.

He's on his knees at one point and leans toward one man. With a finger under the guy's chin, Adrian draws him in, looking every bit like he's going to kiss him within an inch of his life. At the last possible second, though, he grins, swipes his thumb over the man's lower lip, and pulls away.

The man drops back into his seat, a hand on his chest. I swear to God, I can hear him having palpitations. Or maybe that's me. I'm not even at the stage, and I'm breathing hard like it was me who he drew in and let go at the last moment.

Adrian teases another customer, and leaves that one panting for more too.

Looking deliciously self-satisfied, Adrian turns, and he scans the crowd for another victim, and—

His eyes meet mine.

He freezes but only for a beat. Long enough for recognition to unmistakably register on his face before he recovers and zeroes in on his next customer.

This one has his back right to me. Adrian grabs him—his shirt, by the looks of it—and pulls him in. He curves his long fingers around the back of the guy's neck, and he tilts his own head like he's moving in for a kiss.

And when he does, when it absolutely looks like he's locked lips with the man, Adrian's eyes—heavy lidded and smoky-lined and so beautiful—fix right on me. The music drowns out the whimper that escapes my mouth, but barely.

He lets the man go, winks at me, and continues driving everyone wild. This time, he goes for the pole. Oh, Jesus. I can see why he got this job. When his ankles are around the top and he curls his torso up, that not-quite-six-pack is suddenly very, very there. Every muscle stands out, rippling under his skin and the dragon that isn't hidden at all by these shorts.

I take a swig of Coke, but it's about as effective as chugging hot sand. I'm completely mesmerized. The way he moves is so deliciously hypnotic—smooth and sensual, drawing attention to his shoulders, his ass, his abs, and his package. Like the dancer before him, he makes it look easy, but when his muscles tense and quiver with the exertion, it isn't like a spotlight accidentally illuminating a safety net or a piano wire. Quite the contrary—it just underscores how powerful and controlled he is. How utterly sexy his lean, chiseled body really is.

All too soon, the song is over.

Instantly, several hands shoot out with offers. I'm admittedly jealous of whoever gets to accompany him into one of those private booths. I wonder if they have enough money and charm to negotiate one of his other services.

At least Adrian knows I'm here. If he wants to talk to me, he will when he's finished. If not, well... Then it's back to the bus station.

Adrian leaves the stage, and a moment later, he's disappearing through that door, followed by a flustered-looking man with a combover. My toes curl. I'm envious but remind myself to be patient. They won't be back there forever.

I watch the next couple of dancers without much interest. They're sexy, of course, but my mind is fixated on their coworker. I didn't even come here for the purpose of flirting with him or trying to get him into bed. I'd just needed to *see* him.

And I saw him. My God, did I ever.

I shiver at the thought. Now that I've watched him dance, and now that I've got that fake kiss burned into my memory, all I can think of is how much I want him. It should be *illegal* to be as hot as Adrian.

"What are you doing here?"

His voice startles me, and I nearly drop what's left of my drink.

Our eyes meet as he comes closer. He's not hostile—not like he thinks I'm stalking him or something—but there's some definite curiosity in his eyes. Maybe some nerves, too. Like he's not sure what to make of this.

*Join the club, dude.*

I clear my throat. "I came to see you." Which under normal circumstances probably sounded fine, but I realize a second too late that when the guy in question is a stripper, it sounds a bit creepy. "To talk to you, I mean."

"Oh." He dabs at some sweat on his forehead with a dark towel. "What about?"

"I..." I avoid his eyes just so I can pull myself together. "I wanted to take you out to dinner. As a thank you."

"Max." He lowers the towel, and his voice is soft. "You've only got so much cash. I don't want you spending it on me."

"I know. But I didn't feel right leaving without doing something. I just…" I run a hand through my hair. When did I start sweating? "I sat there for almost two hours, hemming and hawing about it, and I couldn't leave. Not yet." Lowering my hand, I look him in the eye. "I didn't come here to perv on you. I just…don't feel like I've thanked you nearly enough."

He smiles, and it's a little shy. His eyes flick toward the stage where one of his coworkers is shimmying up the pole. There's some pink in Adrian's cheeks, though it's probably more from dancing than blushing. Fixing his gaze on his hands, he absently plays with the towel. "I hope it wasn't weird, seeing me dance like that."

"Weird? Oh my God, no. You're…"

He looks at me through his lashes.

I moisten my lips. "You're amazing to watch."

This time, he's definitely blushing. "Thanks." The silence threatens to get awkward, but then he playfully says, "As long as you're here, you want a dance?"

My tongue sticks to the roof of my mouth. "Like…" I nod toward the stage.

Adrian smirks and shakes his head. "No. More like…" He nods toward the private booths.

"Are you serious?"

He shrugs, turning a bit shy again. "It's okay if you don't want—"

"No! Oh my God. No, I'm not saying that. Just… I don't have any money. Besides, you know—"

"This one's on the house." He lifts his eyebrows again. "If you want it, I mean."

*Like you wouldn't believe.*

Mute, I nod.

Adrian takes my hand. His palm is hot and a little damp, but probably not for the same reason mine is. If he notices, he doesn't let on.

He leads me past the bouncer and the neon sign, and we walk down a hallway lined with curtain-covered doorways. The music is even louder back here. Loud enough to rattle my fillings.

Loud enough, I realize with a sprinkle of goose bumps, that two people could fuck each other senseless in one of these booths without being heard.

As if I'm not already getting painfully hard.

At the very last booth, he pulls the curtain back and motions for me to go inside. There's a chair, which I expect. I half expect him to whip the curtain shut and, now that we have some privacy, demand to know why the fuck I'm here.

But he doesn't.

He shuts the curtain and gestures at the chair.

Pulse thumping, I take a seat.

"You ever done this before?" His voice is low and smooth, just loud enough to carry over the music and my heart.

I nod. "It's been a while." And I don't remember being this nervous the first time.

"So you know the rules." He grins as he slides a knee between my thighs and leans over it. "I can touch you, but you can't touch me."

*Please touch me. Please.*

I nod.

Adrian grins. I press back against the seat, not to escape him but to keep from melting onto the floor. His hands start on my forearms and drift up to my shoulders, leaving more goose bumps in their wake.

Seeing his body work and his muscles tense from far away is hot. Feeling it is another thing entirely. Every time he moves—rubbing up against me, turning around and pressing his firm ass against my cock, undulating right in front of my face—I can feel it, and it has never been this difficult to keep my hands off someone. I want to slide them all over his body. Not just his cock or his ass, but everywhere. The planes of his shoulder blades. That tattoo above his hip. The swells and contours of painstakingly toned muscles. His *skin*. I'm sure it's smooth and hot, and I have to curl my fingers into the armrest to keep from finding out.

"My God, Adrian." I gaze up at him, breathing hard. "You're so fucking beautiful."

He smiles, equal parts wicked and sweet, and slides his hot, strong hands up my chest. I have never in my life wished harder for a shirt to evaporate into thin air.

Adrian moves in like he might kiss me, and even though I know that's a tease he loves to employ, my heart still skips when his lips are suddenly out of my reach. I let go of a frustrated groan, and he grinds harder against me. He's keeping perfect time with the music, sending my pulse all over the place, and has my head spinning faster and faster with every touch. I've been turned on during dances before, but never like this. Never like I might skip right over an orgasm and go straight to spontaneous combustion.

He leans in and exhales, letting his breath caress my neck.

"Oh my God…"

He does it again. Then his lips brush my ear, and he whispers, "I'm glad you're here."

I gulp, trying not to just burst into flames. "M-me too."

Adrian pushes himself up, forearms resting on my shoulders, and gazes down at me. His body is still moving to the music, but more subtly now. Like it's an unconscious thing, or an afterthought, and his attention is elsewhere.

Elsewhere as in…on me.

He shifts a little, and with fingers that I swear are trembling, he smooths my hair. I shiver. So does he.

I swallow hard again. "How negotiable is that rule about touching you?"

"According to the owner of the club? It's not." He makes a slow, deliberate gesture of licking his lips. "But he's not here."

"So you're making the rules."

Adrian nods, eyes never leaving mine. "Yeah. And I…won't tell anyone if you break that one."

"Is that an invitation?"

He just holds my gaze, hot skin still burning against my clothes.

I stare back at him for a few long, tense beats.

Then, praying like hell that I'm not crossing any lines, I reach up and touch his face.

Adrian closes his eyes. He presses into my hand. "That wasn't what I was expecting."

I turn my hand over and stroke his cheek with the backs of my fingers. "What were you expecting?"

Our eyes meet again. I give his face another soft stroke.

Then Adrian grasps the back of my neck, leans down, and presses his lips to mine.

# Chapter 9
## Adrian

Everything is completely still.

The room is vibrating from the music, but the rest of the world disappears, and it's just us. Just Max. Just me. Just that soft point of contact between his lips and mine.

His hand drifts from my face up into my hair. The other arm slowly snakes around my waist and draws me closer. Not pinning me or trying to immobilize me, but letting me sink against him.

I nudge his lips with mine, and they part without protest, so I tease them with the tip of my tongue. He opens eagerly, and the kiss deepens, his mouth welcoming my tongue as a soft groan escapes his throat.

And he holds me. Really, really holds me. I'm almost naked, and our erections are brushing against each other, and I would expect any other man—especially a total stranger—to start getting more handsy. Squeezing my ass. Playing with a nipple. *Something.*

But he doesn't. He's obviously turned on—those little moans and the way he shivers every time our cocks brush are a dead giveaway—but he's not groping.

My God, I want him. The more he kisses me and holds me like this, the more I want to take him home, rip off his clothes, and fuck until neither of us can move. The more we're gentle and unhurried, the more I want to turn him loose and see how rough and desperate he can be.

*I know you can control yourself. Now show me what happens when you let go.*

I press my erection against his, and he breaks the kiss with a gasp. Our foreheads touch, and we're both breathing hard. Both shaking a little.

"For the record," he says, his voice barely carrying over the music, "this isn't what I came here for." He slides a hand down my back, then up again. "Not that I'm complaining."

I grin and kiss him again. I have every intention of saying something witty, but when his fingers curve around the back of my neck and he lifts his hips to press back against my cock, speech fails me. Except damn it, I want him touching me all over, and he's still holding back. Still keeping himself from groping. At the start, I appreciated it, but now I'm impatient and frustrated.

I break away again, and in between gulps of air, I murmur, "I thought you wanted to touch me."

"I do."

"Then"—I take his wrist and move his hand to my ass—"*touch me.*"

I'm not even sure who groans this time. Quite possibly both of us. His other hand follows suit, and as we kiss again, he kneads my ass through my shorts. Our cocks keep rubbing together, and his body heat radiates through his clothes and makes me dizzy. Or maybe that's his kiss. Or the fact that I keep forgetting to breathe unless it's to take in a deep whiff of his masculine scent.

Somewhere around the edges of my consciousness, I remember he's supposed to be on his way back to California and I'm supposed to be working. That he came here to buy me a dinner he can't afford to thank me for the thousandth time.

But that's all scrambled and hazy now. All I want is him, and all I can think about is how much he turns me on. Everything else can be dealt with later. For right now, I've got my hands and body and mouth on the man I wasn't so sure I'd ever see again. It doesn't have to make sense. It is, and I'm not doing a damn thing to stop it.

I touch my forehead to his. "Would I have to twist your arm to convince you to stay with me another night?"

His hands slide up and down my thighs. "Absolutely not."

"Maybe you could sleep in my bed this time."

Max groans softly, lifting his chin enough for his lips to graze mine. "One condition."

"Hmm?"

"You're not sleeping on the couch."

I laugh as a delicious shudder ripples through me. "Deal." I rock my hips back and forth, and when he curses, I lean in and whisper in his ear, "Can't promise either of us will be sleeping, though."

His fingers press into my thighs, and then his hands slide around to cup my ass again as he growls, "I don't want to sleep. I just want you."

Oh, sweet Jesus.

"We should get out of here."

He tilts his head back enough to meet my gaze, and his expression is suddenly serious. "Your job, though. Don't you—"

I kiss him softly. "I almost never ask to cut out early. My boss will let me go."

"Are you sure?"

I sit back a bit and gaze down at him. Then, as I slide my palms up his chest, I nod. "Yeah. I'm sure."

He licks his lips as he lets his gaze drift down my torso. "Those shorts don't fit you quite so well when you're turned on."

"No, they don't." I try to ignore the growing discomfort, but now that he's mentioned it, I definitely notice. Cursing softly, I adjust myself. Not that it helps. "Occupational hazard."

"Uh-huh." He cups my cock and balls through the straining shorts, and I shudder so hard I have to grab his shoulders for balance. "Kind of seems like I should do something about this."

I bite my lip and moan. A response forms on the tip of my tongue, but then his thumb traces over the head of my cock, and I don't even remember what language I speak. All that comes out is a throaty, "Ungh…"

He makes quick work of the top button, and the zipper pretty much comes undone on its own, freeing my painfully hard cock. Then he's stroking me, and he's kissing his way up my midsection, it's all I can do not to cry out with pure pleasure.

This is so against the rules. My boss would have a fit if he knew I was letting a customer touch me. Some other clubs allow all kinds of things in the back room, but not this guy.

Still, I can't tell Max no. I can't do anything except rock into his grip and card my fingers through his soft hair. "God, yeah…"

He curves a hand under my thigh and nudges me upward. "Sit up."

"Hmm?"

"Up?"

I do without thinking, and suddenly his lips are around my cock. I freeze for a second, wanting to warn him that I'm probably sweating, but he obviously doesn't care. He licks up and down my cock, then around the head, and now I'm gripping his hair for dear life as he makes my heart race and the room spin. He steadies my cock with one hand, and the other cups my ass cheek, and I swear he's encouraging me to fuck his mouth, so I do. And he groans. Oh fuck. The vibration of his voice is as intense as the wet heat of his lips and tongue. In my mind's eye, I'm already coming, shooting my load down his eager throat, and holy shit, I'm almost there for real.

"Oh yeah," I moan, watching my cock slide in and out of his mouth. "Oh yeah, I'm...so close. So... *Fuck*." Every muscle in my body tenses. He must feel it, because he doubles down and gives me even more, and thank God for the hand on my ass, or I'd have tumbled right off the chair with that first violent shudder. He holds me up, though, keeping me as still as possible and not letting my cock slide from his mouth until he's swallowed every drop of cum.

When I finally slump over him, he eases me down into his lap, and he's holding me again. Stroking my hair. Supporting my boneless, shaking body.

He's still hard, but he's not pushing me to do anything about it. Is he that easygoing, or have I been sleeping with jackasses my whole life? Maybe it's just been so long since I've been with someone who doesn't handle me like a semi-sentient blowup doll, I've forgotten what tenderness feels like. I don't even know. I just know I like the way he does things.

I use the back of the chair to lift myself up enough to meet his gaze. Smiling, Max touches my cheek again. I turn my head enough to kiss the middle of his palm before. "We should get out of here."

Max nods. "Ready whenever you are."

~*~

My boss isn't thrilled to let me cut out for the night, but even he admits I hardly abuse the privilege, so he lets me go. I leave Max in the lounge area while I change clothes, and minutes later, we're on our way out.

"It's a bit of a walk to my car," I tell him as we head toward the strip. "I park at the casino even when I'm only working here."

"Why's that?"

"Because at least that lot has decent security. Every time I park here, something gets ripped off." I slide my hands into the pockets of my jeans. "Not that I keep a whole lot in my car that's worth stealing, but…"

"No, I can understand that. And I don't mind walking."

We turn onto the main drag, and I lead him down the route I've walked so many times I could do it in my sleep. In fact, it's so automatic that I don't even think twice until we start wading through a thick crowd, and I realize where we are—in front of the Bellagio fountain.

It looks different out here because it's not in the middle of the night. It's dark out, but there's a ton of people, and I can tell by the way the crowd is swelling and everyone is vying for position against the railing that they're waiting for the fountain to start its show.

But still, this is it. This is the place where I met Max.

Wondering if he's noticed, I glance at him.

His features are tight, and… Yeah, I'm pretty sure he notices.

I touch his arm. "You all right?"

He nods. Then he turns to me, and a soft smile forms. "Just thinking about the last time I was here."

"Me too."

He swallows, and neither of us say anything as we work our way through a particularly dense part of the crowd. When we have some breathing room again, he says, "I can't even tell you how many times I watched those fountains from here. And from"—he nods toward the towering hotel beyond the pools—"there."

"That's where you stayed?"

"Yeah." To my surprise, he laughs quietly and shakes his head. "You know the TVs in the room will play the music so you can watch from your window and get the whole experience?"

"No shit? Really?"

Chuckling, he nods. "Yeah." Slowly, though, the amusement fades, and he keeps his eyes down as we continue through the crowd. "I kind of wish I hadn't listened to it."

"Why's that?"

He motions toward the fountain. "Because when I was out here, it reminded me that I used to be up there."

"Wow. That must've been…" Fuck, what was the word? *Are* there words to describe listening to the same music from a luxury hotel room, then on the street less than a week later?

Vegas. That's the only word I can think of. It's so quintessentially *Vegas*.

And as if on cue, that music kicks on. Lights come to life, and the fountains start shooting water skyward. I fully expect Max to walk even faster, but he slows. Then he stops. And through a hole in the crowd, he watches the fountains while I watch him.

He's not an easy guy to read anyway, and right now, I couldn't tell you what he's thinking if my life depended on it. His expression is blank, if still a little tight. The dancing water reflects in his eyes, and all I can think is that it feels like a lifetime has gone by since we met here. No one could possibly look at him and know he was once huddled against one of these concrete planters with a four-day beard, a cardboard sign, and a change cup.

*I almost walked right by you.*

The thought takes my breath away. Despite being out in public, I slip my hand into his. Max glances down at our hands. Then he turns to me, the bright lights from the show casting a warm, gold light on his face, and he smiles.

He closes some of the space between us, and his other hand comes up to caress my cheek just like he did when I told him he could break the no touching rule. I swallow. We're surrounded by people, but I feel like we're as alone as we were that first night. In completely different states of mind, no longer strangers, but still the only two people standing on this long stretch of concrete beside the water.

I don't know what to say, only that it feels like something should be said. It's impossible to think, though. Everything about us is so surreal. This doesn't even feel like real life.

Except it is. And somehow, I stopped the other night. And somehow, he came back to me. And now…

*You're here. I'm here. What now?*

As if he can read my mind, Max wraps an arm around my waist, and right there on the street, he draws me in and kisses me. Just like in the club, he's gentle and sweet, and now that we're both standing, I like how it feels to be smaller than him. He's not huge—not even the biggest guy I've ever made out with—but there's something broad and safe and sheltering about him, and I think I could get lost in it.

A shoulder smacks against the middle of my back, knocking me into Max and both of us nearly off our feet, and the moment is over. The muttered "Fags" tells me it was not accidental.

Max rights me, glaring after the asshole. "Just when you think we've made progress as a species."

"No shit. At least neither of us cut a lip or lost a tooth." I shake myself and turn his chin so he's looking at me. "Anyway. Let's just get out of here."

He's still annoyed but softens and gestures in the direction we'd been heading. "After you."

# Chapter 10
## Max

"Before we get too carried away," Adrian says on the way up his porch steps, "I could really use a shower. I'm disgusting."

I chuckle. "I disagree on that last part, but I won't stop you."

He glances over his shoulder and smirks. "I was hoping you'd join me."

"Don't have to twist my arm for that either."

"Good." He opens the storm door, and his keys jingle for a second before one of them crunches in the lock. Then he pushes the main door open and we walk inside. After we're closed in and the deadbolt is turned, he faces me, slides his hands into my front pockets, and tugs me to him. "I swear, if it had taken us another two minutes to get here, we'd be doing this on the side of the road."

I wrap my arms around him and kiss him. "Sounds kinky."

Adrian laughs, shaking his head. "You're a dork. Come on."

He lets me go and leads me back into his bedroom and then into the master bathroom. As soon as he starts peeling off his T-shirt, my blood starts rushing south. He's all mine tonight? How is this possible?

No point in questioning it—I'm going to enjoy every minute of this and every inch of him.

So I quickly strip out of my own clothes, and a moment later, we're in the narrow shower together. I can't decide if I want to stare at him and drink in the sight of his lean, naked body, or if I want to press my own naked body against his. The close confines pretty much make the latter a foregone conclusion—there's barely enough room for both of us to stand, never mind leer at each other. What a shame.

He kisses me as we wrap our arms around each other. Hot water runs over and between us, and my hands follow the streams down his torso. This is hardly the first time I've been naked with a man, but it's my first time naked with Adrian, and I don't know if it'll be the last, so I intend to memorize every line of his body.

Getting clean is still a priority too, and somehow he manages to make even that sexy. Bar of soap in hand, he turns around and presses back against me, and I kiss his neck and knead his hips as he soaps himself up. He guides my hands into the lather, and my slippery palms glide all over him. Above his hip on his right side, there's a thick ridge, which I assume is his tattoo. Sometimes they have raised edges, though this one seems more pronounced. Or maybe I'm just that hyperaware of every line and divot of his beautiful topography.

Adrian presses back harder, rubbing his ass over my erection. God, I can't wait to fuck him. Or let him fuck me. I haven't even figured out if he's a top or a bottom, or if he's vers, but I can't think of any configuration that would be disappointing. As much as I want to bury myself inside him and drive him into the mattress until he comes again like he did at the strip club, I won't say no if he wants to do the same to me. In fact, the thought makes me shiver.

He looked over his shoulder, then turns around. "Sorry. I'm hogging the water."

"You're fine."

"Still…" He squeezes past me, and now I have the bulk of the hot water. It does feel good—the novelty of a hot shower has absolutely not worn off—but not as good as Adrian, so I draw him back in against me and kiss him. He doesn't protest. And dear God, he's as hard as he was at the club. How he fits that thing into his tiny shorts, I'll never know, but it's free now, and pressed right up against mine.

I cup his perfect ass in both hands, this time without the layer of leather in the way. Now I definitely regret not flirting with him a little harder at his table—if I'd known what he was hiding under that dress shirt and tie, I'd never have been able to play blackjack. I don't imagine I'll ever play it again without thinking about long fingers on cards and black hair tumbling into blue eyes and flawless, powerful muscles on a slender frame.

I draw back to meet his gaze. Some of his hair is plastered to his forehead, and I brush it out of the way. His eye makeup is smeared, but it just makes his eyes look even bluer and brighter.

"I'm serious," I whisper. "You're fucking beautiful."

He laughs a little and blushes. "Thank you." Sliding his arms around my neck, he lifts himself up to kiss me softly. "You're not so bad yourself, you know."

I just grin and kiss him again, letting it linger. And linger. And linger some more. Open-mouthed, breathless, hands all over bodies and bodies rubbing together—I could kiss like this all fucking night.

Adrian breaks away this time, and those blue eyes are on fire now. "We should really take this into the bedroom."

"Good idea."

He shuts off the water. Without the rush of the shower, my pounding heart is the loudest thing in the room. My hands are unsteady and more than a little clumsy as I dry off, but I manage.

After we drape our towels over the shower curtain rod, I follow him into the bedroom. He pauses to pull a bottle of lube and some condoms out of the nightstand drawer. Oh fuck yes.

Then he throws back the covers, climbs into bed, and beckons for me to do the same.

"You were right about this bed." I move across the firm, even mattress to press myself against him. "It *is* more comfortable than the couch."

Adrian puts his arms around my neck as we come together for a kiss. "Told you." We both laugh between kisses, and this is… My God, it's just perfect. My body is absolutely vibrating with need for his, and I want us to be fucking and coming and losing our minds, but I'm still not over the relief of just having him in my arms in the first place. If all we do tonight is kiss, even with a condom well within reach, I'll be a happy man come sunrise.

Somehow, he's on his back now, and I'm on top. He takes full advantage, too, and he runs his hands all over me like I did to him before. Up and down my back. Into my hair. Down my sides. Over my ass. He drags his nails up my back, and I gasp hard enough to break the kiss. As soon as I do, he starts on my neck, and I cradle his head in my hand, damp hair between my fingers as his lips skate all over my throat. When I close my fingers enough to pull, he moans, then bites the side of my neck, and we both shudder.

"God," he breathes beneath my ear. "This is really happening right?" He pushes his hips up so our dicks rub together. "I'm not dreaming again?"

"Again?" I lift up so I can see his face. "You telling me you've dreamed about this before?"

Eyes locked on mine, he sweeps his tongue across his lips. "If I say I have, will you do what you did in my dream?"

"Hmm, that depends. What did I do?"

He rakes his nails over my ass cheeks, grinning when I grunt softly. "You fucked me until I cried."

A shiver pushes all the breath out of my lungs. "Cried in a good way, I hope?"

"Oh yeah. Of course I woke up before I came, but I have a feeling it would've been *awesome*."

I lean down and kiss just above his collarbone. "Guess we'll have to see how it ends for real, won't we?"

He arches under me, whimpering softly. "Please?"

"How did I fuck you in your dream? Position, I mean?"

He squirms some more. "Hands and knees."

"Hmm." I kiss below his ear and whisper, "Then you better turn over."

We separate, and while I get the condom and lube, he turns onto his hands and knees. Of course, he's impossibly sexy like that, offering up his ass to me. I don't even have the wrapper open yet, and I already can't wait.

I move behind him and put the condom and bottle aside. Then I take his ass cheeks in my hands and push them apart, and run my tongue along the crack.

"Holy—" He bucks against me, and when I do it again, he makes a choked sound.

"Like that?" I ask.

"Yeah. Ungh. God."

I grin, then go in for more. I tease his hole with my tongue, alternately circling and probing, and he presses back against me as if looking for more. It's been ages since I've done this, never mind with someone as enthusiastic and vocal, and I can't get enough. Not when he's moaning and squirming like that every time I touch him. Fuck him till he cries? Sign me the hell up.

I keep one hand on his ass and slip the other between his legs. With the lightest possible touch of my fingertips, I tease his balls.

"Max…" He whimpers. "Max, c'mon. Fuck…fuck me."

Oh, I want to, and I will, but his breathless pleading is too hot for words. I keep tonguing him, keep teasing his balls, and he keeps right on whispering my name between moans and shivers.

"Fuck me, damn it," he growls. "C'mon, I want your cock *now*."

I give his hole one last lick and then sit up. I should've put the condom on before, but there isn't much I can do about it now, so I just get it on as quickly as I can.

In front of me, Adrian rocks back and forth like I'm already fucking him, pantomiming how he'll move once he's on my cock. Jesus, I can't wait.

Finally, the condom is on, and I put some lube on it. Then I kneel between his bent legs and guide myself in.

The instant the head brushes his hole, he shudders violently. "Oh God…"

I press against him. Not hard enough to penetrate but enough he knows I'm there. "You want me, Adrian?"

"Uh-huh. Please."

"I'm right here." I trail my fingertips up his spine. "Come and get it."

He arches like a cat under my touch, and then he rocks back against me. "Oh yeah. Fuck." We're teetering right there, right where one slight move from either of us will push me into him. Where he's just beginning to yield, and I'm just beginning to push in, and it's a stalemate, a staring contest, and—

I nudge my hips forward a fraction of an inch, and I'm inside him.

His arms shake under him. The world spins around me. As I withdraw and push in again, we both growl curses and things I doubt either of us can understand.

He starts rocking again, and so do I. Slow and steady were fine and good before, but now I'm eager to be all the way in, and he seems just as eager to have me, and in no time, I'm fucking him deep and hard.

"How's this?" I manage through clenched teeth. "This what I did in your dream?"

Adrian moans, then glances over his shoulder. "Dream-you could learn a lot from real-you."

I grin and ride him as hard as I can, and he meets me thrust for thrust. I so want this to last, but I've been turned on since the strip club, and my need for release is overwhelming. "G-gonna…come…" I dig my fingers into his hips. My body's got a mind of its own now, and I'm not even trying to fight off my orgasm anymore. "God, you feel so… Oh yeah…"

"Yeah," he murmurs. "Come. Lemme… I want to hear—"

Anything else he says is drowned out when I slam all the way into him, throw my head back, and roar. And Adrian, he doesn't stop. He takes over and swivels his hips or…or *something*, and he keeps me coming and coming until I swear I black out for a couple of seconds.

When the smoke clears, we're down on the mattress. He's sunk onto his stomach, and I'm slumped over him. I don't remember dropping like this, but I guess it's just as well because I doubt I can hold myself up. It's all I can do to pull out.

In between gasps for air, I kiss the back of his neck. "Still…gotta make you come."

He laughs softly. "You can catch your breath first. It's okay."

"Okay." I kiss his sweat-dampened skin again. "Gimme a sec."

It only takes a minute or so, and I can finally move. I push myself up. "Get on your back. I'm going to get rid of this, and then I'm going to make sure you come as hard as I did."

"I love the sound of that."

As I get up and he rolls over, we exchange grins. I pause for a kiss, then force my wobbly legs to carry me into the bathroom. After the condom is gone and I've quickly washed my hands, I come back, and I'm greeted with the sexiest sight imaginable—Adrian, naked and sweaty, stretched out on his back, slowly stroking his cock.

"Oh wow." I lick my lips. "That's something I could watch all night."

"Don't watch." He beckons to me. "This is audience participation."

I laugh as I slide in next to him, and as soon as we're close enough, I kiss him. "Tell me how you want me to get you off," I whisper. "I can give you head, or you can fuck me, or—"

"Just like this." His other hand drifts up into my hair and pulls me back to his lips. "I love the way you kiss," he murmurs. "Turns… Turns me on."

I'm more than happy to oblige and kiss him deeply. He's breathing faster, sharper, like he's getting close. I want to do more, so I reach down, and while he strokes himself, I tease his balls. That earns me a low, delicious moan, and he kisses me even harder.

Without breaking the kiss, I shift a little so I'm partway over him. Then I move my hand farther between his legs. He parts them as if he knows exactly what I have in mind, and as soon as my fingertips meet his slick hole, he exhales hard through his nose and bucks his hips against my hand. I grin into his kiss and slide two fingers inside him. He clenches around them, and when I bend them to stroke his prostate, he shudders again.

We kiss, and he pumps his cock, and I finger him, and every breath he takes is sharper than the last until he's shaking all over, tense and squirming, moaning into my kiss.

He breaks the kiss with a harsh "Fuck!" and lets his head fall back to the pillow. I kiss up and down his neck, and the hand in my hair holds tight as if to say *don't you dare stop doing exactly what you're doing.* His pulse pounds against my lips. Every time he speaks or moans, the vibration drives me wild.

He clamps down even harder on my fingers, arches off the bed, and releases the most deliciously helpless cry as he comes, and I don't stop until he sinks back to the bed with a satiated sigh.

"Holy fuck," he breathes. "That was awesome."

"Uh-huh." I carefully withdraw my fingers, then prop myself up on my elbow. When our eyes meet, the remaining smudges of eyeliner are just slightly wetter than before. "Looks like I did fuck you hard enough to make you cry."

He wipes his eyes and inspects his thumb. "I'll be damned. Guess you did." We both laugh as I lean in for another kiss. After a moment he meets my gaze again. "For what it's worth," he says, "I would've been glad you came back even if we hadn't ended up like this."

"Yeah. Me too. But…I'm not going to complain about this part either."

He chuckles. "Neither am I."

"I was serious, by the way. About taking you to dinner."

"You don't have to." He combs his fingers through my hair. "Besides, I could use your help getting through the rest of that pizza."

I laugh and press a kiss to his forehead. "I'm happy to help with that."

# Chapter 11
## Adrian

I definitely wasn't expecting to spend tonight kicked back in my living room with Max, some cold pizza, and the satisfied ache of some spectacular sex. This is, to say the least, a pleasant surprise.

After a while, Max gets a little quiet, though. He's staring off into space, and the creases in his forehead are hard to miss.

"You okay?"

He nods as he turns to me. "Just thinking about tomorrow. It's… You know, back to the bus station and onward to L.A."

"Ah. Right." The disappointment setting up shop in my stomach kills my appetite. I set my plate on the coffee table next to my Coke, pull my feet up under me on the couch, and try to look more relaxed than I feel. "Does your friend know you're still here tonight?"

He shakes his head. "No, I told him I'd give him a call when I got there. He's expecting me in the next day or two, but…" Max shrugs. "It probably wouldn't hurt to give him a call, though. I can't imagine he thinks I'm going to stay here very long." Maybe it's my imagination, but I swear there's a note of sadness in his voice.

"You can use my phone if you need to." I gesture toward the kitchen. "*Mi casa, su casa.*"

Max smiles, though his eyes definitely don't echo it. "Thanks." He wipes his hands on a napkin, then stands. "I should go ahead and do that."

I watch him go into the kitchen.

"Hey, Greg," his voice carries into the living room. "Yeah, it's Max. Listen, I'm in Vegas for one more night. No, everything's fine. Just, uh… Just didn't make it to the bus station yet."

I pick up my Coke and take a swallow. Part of me wants to get offended that he's being so cagey about why he's still here, but that's ridiculous. What's he going to tell his friend? He decided to stick around and bang his stripper friend for one more night?

My own thoughts make me roll my eyes. With almost anyone else, I could believe that. I've had enough men treat me as a masturbation aid that it doesn't even surprise me anymore when they don't. In fact, it *does* surprise me when I'm in bed with someone who seems to really want to be there with me. Not just the nearest warm, willing body. Not just the guy who can turn himself inside out on a pole. *Me.*

I cut my eyes toward the kitchen, and a lump rises in my throat. I spent this evening in bed with a guy like that. Chances are, we'll spend the rest of the night like that.

And then…tomorrow…

He'll be gone.

Just like he was supposed to be gone today. Something tells me letting him go is going to be even harder tomorrow than it was earlier. My heart sinks. What was I thinking? If seeing him off was so fucking difficult already, what in the world made me think it was a good idea to get in bed with him before seeing him off *again*?

Except I *hadn't* thought it was a good idea. I hadn't been thinking at all about seeing him off. I'd only been thinking about how much I wanted him and how addictive it was to see all that need and hunger in his eyes, knowing it was directed at *me*. It didn't even matter—and still doesn't—that this is probably just him needing to say thanks for the past couple of days. And I appreciate that part. I do. I just wish it didn't make me a delusional idiot to hope there's something else going on here.

He's about to get back on his feet. The proverbial phoenix rising up from his own ashes. I doubt he wants to get his fresh start with someone like me attached to his side.

I glance at my pizza again. Nope. Definitely not hungry anymore.

In the kitchen, Max wraps up his call, and a second later, he comes back into the living room. "Okay. That's taken care of." He sits on the couch beside me. "He says he might have a couple of leads for me too. For jobs."

"Oh. That's good." I smile despite my own stupid emotions.

"Nothing spectacular," he adds as he pulls another slice from the pizza box. "But if something pans out, it'll be a damn good start."

"I'm glad to hear it." I pause. "Are you still planning to sell everything you have in storage?"

Max nods. "I'll go through it and pull out anything I need or that has some kind of sentimental value, but most of it's gotta go. I need some quick cash." He stares at the pizza in his hand for a moment, then sets it on his plate without taking a bite. "I figure if I can get my hands on a cheap car, at least I can get around. And...have a place to sleep."

I sit up. "You're going to sleep in your *car*?"

Max shrugs like his shoulders are suddenly heavier than they should be. "Have you seen how much rent is in Los Angeles? I can stay at my buddy's house for a little while, but..."

I stare at him in horror.

He meets my gaze and smiles as he pats my leg. "It's not as bad as it sounds. All I have to do is get a cheap gym membership, and I've got access to a shower. It's a temporary fix." He shrugs again, a little more easily this time. "If I can get some decent money for my stuff, maybe I won't have to go that route, but I'm not above it."

I can't stomach the idea of Max sleeping in his car. He's already been homeless once. A car isn't much of a step up. But what can I do?

Before I can think twice, I blurt out, "Maybe I could help you with your stuff. Sorting it and getting it sold, I mean." My stomach somersaults, but I ignore it. "With two people, it might be faster, you know?"

He holds my gaze. "You'd...really?"

I nod. "And I could drive. So, you know, you wouldn't have to deal with the bus, and you'd have a way to get around. I can't stay very long, but...like a few days? A week, tops?" Now that I've said it, I feel like an idiot. Why would he want me to tag along with him? And why am I hoping so hard that he'll take me up on it?

"I'd..." He clears his throat. "I would *love* to have your company, but I mean... I can't ask more than you've already done."

"Max." I sit up and slide a hand over his knee, still marveling at how easy it is for us to touch. "I didn't want to leave you out on the street, and I don't like the idea of leaving you to live out of your car. If having me there to sort your stuff and sell it will help prevent that from happening? Then I *want* to." I hold his gaze. *I also want a reason to be where you are anyway, and I don't care how pathetic that is.*

He looks down at my hand. I almost draw it back, but then he puts his on top of it and squeezes. "You really are amazing. You know that?"

I smile and turn my hand over under his so I can lace our fingers together. "I just want you to be okay."

"I will be." He looks at our hands again, watching his thumb run back and forth along mine. "And one of these days, I *will* make all this up to you."

*I don't care.* "I know."

He chews his lip. For a while, neither of us says anything. Finally, he meets my gaze. "Are you sure it won't cause you problems at one of your jobs?"

My heart speeds up. "Yeah. I don't take a lot of time off, so when I want to, they're flexible. If you can wait one more day, I can work tomorrow, and then I should be good to go."

Max is hesitant, but after a moment, he smiles. "Thank you. And yeah, I don't mind waiting another day. As long as you need, really."

I try not to let it show that I'm getting excited at the prospect of spending a few more days with him. "Let me call my bosses. See what they say."

He nods. Then he uses my hand to pull me closer, and he cups my face as he kisses me softly. "Oh, one more thing."

"Hmm?"

"When we hit the road..." He grins. "We should probably take the rest of those condoms with us."

I just shiver.

~*~

I'm not one for taking vacation. It's not that I'm a workaholic or don't have a life, but my schedule tends to work out so I have two or three days off at a time anyway. I prefer to save those days in case there's an emergency or I want to take a long trip somewhere, so my bosses usually have to badger me into using up my time.

Today, that pays off. Both of my bosses ask me to come in tomorrow since it's such short notice, and after that, they'll make sure my shifts are covered for a few days.

I feel bad for holding Max up for an extra day—or a little more, considering we won't leave until the following afternoon—but he insists it's fine. After all, it gives him a chance to follow up on some of the leads his friend found for him.

In fact, by the time I come home the next night, Max has two interviews lined up in Los Angeles. They're not quite what he was hoping for—not that I understand the ins and outs of his industry—but they're steady paychecks. Little by little, things are looking up for him, and I hope it continues like this. He deserves better.

It's mid-afternoon on Friday when I'm finally awake, caffeinated, and ready to roll. Max is still kind of bleary-eyed too; his sleep pattern's all kinds of fucked-up, and spending the wee hours of the morning having sex with me probably doesn't help. He's not complaining, though. Neither am I.

Before I know it, Las Vegas is a dusty blur in the rearview, and we're out in the open desert.

"You want me to drive for a while," he says, "just say so."

"I'll let you know. It's not that long of a drive, though."

"It's four and a half hours."

"I know. But I used to drive all the way to Denver from here without stopping except to get gas." I shrug. "I can handle this."

"What was in Denver?"

I suddenly regret mentioning the city. Eyes fixed on the stretch of interstate in front of me, I say, "My ex."

"Oh. I... Sorry. I didn't mean to pry."

"Eh, it's okay. It was a long time ago." I fidget in the driver's seat. "Almost four years, now that I think about it."

"How long were you together?"

"Two. He was a dental student when I met him. There's a dental school in Vegas that's one of the best in the country or something. I guess. Anyway, he was a few months away from graduating when we met, and we decided to do the long distance thing after he moved to Denver."

Max says nothing, but the question is buzzing in the air.

"He...changed his mind when he figured out it would hurt his chances of establishing a respectable practice if people found out about me."

"What?" Max makes an exasperated noise. "Denver's pretty progressive. I can't imagine people would be that weirded out over a gay dentist."

"A gay—" I glance at him. "No, it wasn't because he's gay. It was because I'm a stripper."

"Oh. Right." He rolls his eyes, then turns to me. "People really get that weird over you being a stripper?"

"That weird and weirder. Especially if they're dating me."

"Seriously?"

I nod. "Either they decide I'm an embarrassment or a liability, or they figure they're too good for me. I'm fine for some bedroom entertainment for a while, but anything more than that?" I shake my head. Then I exhale. "I'm sorry. You don't need to hear—"

"No, it's okay. I just can't believe people are that dismissive of you just because you're a stripper." Beat. "Okay, I can, only because I know how people are about sex workers. I just..." He's quiet, and he's watching me so intently I want to squirm. "I just can't fathom someone feeling that way about *you*."

I laugh bitterly. "You'd be surprised."

Max says nothing, but he's still watching me.

The scrutiny makes me squirm. "Everything you said before about sex workers and coal miners makes sense, but in practice, it doesn't work that way. Once you start taking off your clothes for money, you're a lower class of human being who isn't worth the effort it takes to date.

L.A. WITT

Still worth texting for a hookup, but anything beyond that?" I shake my head again. "Forget it. And once you let it slip you're willing to have sex for money? You better be willing to hand out free samples to your friends."

He pushes out a breath and stares out the window. "I know that's how people think. It's just hard to imagine applying it to an actual person."

"It's easier once you stop thinking of someone like me as an actual person."

His head snaps toward me. "Are you kidding? No way." He pauses. "I...never got the impression you're ashamed of what you do."

"I'm not. Not at all." I sigh, adjusting my grip on the wheel since the ache in my fingers tells me I've been holding it a bit tighter than I need to. "But that doesn't mean I'm oblivious to how people feel about what I do."

He doesn't speak. I'm not sure he knows what to say, and maybe there isn't anything to say at this point. Now I feel like shit for making things awkward. He's never treated me badly for what I do, so why should I dump this on him?

In fact, he's the last person I should be dumping it on, because he's the first person to know I'm a stripper-slash-whore and not start looking at me sideways. Not that he knew me for very long before I told him, but still. And in fact, when I gave him a lap dance...

I swallow. "Can I ask you something?"

"Sure." He's guarded, but not horrendously so.

"When we went into the private booth at the club, did you want to sleep with me?"

He's watching me again. "Are you asking if I was attracted to you?"

"I guess. Yeah."

"Of course I was. I had no idea if you were interested in me, or if I registered on your radar at all, but...yeah. I wanted you."

"So when I took you back there, did you think…" I'm not sure how to phrase it without sounding like I'm making an accusation.

"I didn't know what to think," he says. "Honestly, I loved watching you on the stage, and I wanted to see you dance in private too, but I wasn't expecting…what happened."

"Not until I said you could touch me?"

Max shifts a little. "That was about the time I thought we might take things further, yeah."

"Then…" I chew the inside of my cheek.

"Hmm?"

I pull in a deep breath, and glance at him before fixing my attention on the dusty pavement again. "Why did you touch my face?"

"What do you mean?"

"I mean…" Fuck, when did it get so hard to speak? "You had me almost naked in your lap. We were both turned on. I thought you'd grab my ass, or… I don't know. Something. But not that." My cheek tingles at the memory of his unexpected caress. "Why my face?"

He's staring intently out the windshield. I let him think; if it's difficult for me to ask, it's probably tougher for him to formulate an answer.

After a moment, he slides his hand over my thigh, and goose bumps spring up along my forearms. "Look. I'm on the homestretch to forty. I've had plenty of sex in my life. The novelty of touching a man's ass or feeling his hard-on—it's not like I'm sixteen anymore, you know?"

Not sure what to make of that, I steal another glance. First at his face. Then at his hand. And finally back at the road.

"When I asked to touch you," he says softly, "it wasn't because I had a gorgeous piece of ass in my lap and wanted to cop a few feels and maybe fuck." His thumb trails back and forth along the seam of my shorts. "It was because I wanted *you*."

# Chapter 12
## Max

My statement hangs in the air for a long moment. I'm not sure what answer he was expecting, but I'm pretty sure that wasn't it.

And I'm pretty sure I could never explain to him why it's so difficult to restrain myself from telling him to pull over so I can touch him again. More than just my hand on his shorts, I mean. We don't even have to have sex. I just…like the way he feels against my skin, and I like the way I feel when I'm touching him.

The silence is uncomfortable as hell, though. I try not to be conspicuous about watching his face—both because he's gorgeous and because I'm watching for tells that I've overstepped a boundary or something.

Finally, I speak. "I hate blackjack."

"Uh." He eyes me. "Okay?"

"I was in the casino to play baccarat and Texas hold 'em. The only reason I was at your table was because of you."

Adrian's thin black eyebrows jump, and he glances at me again. "What?"

"I saw you when I was on my way to play poker. And I… I had to stop." I laugh at my own stupidity and stare out at the desert. "All that booze, and I still couldn't work up the nerve to flirt with you."

The muscles in his thigh relax slightly under my hand, the tension beginning to melt away. "Really?"

"Yeah. If anything, I'm even more attracted to you now than I was then because I know you. I mean... I don't know much about you. We only really met a few days ago, and... You know what I mean."

Adrian nods wordlessly.

"I do know that you're willing to take in a complete stranger and help him get back on his feet," I go on. "And that you've never once made me feel like the loser I've convinced myself I am. The fact that you strip or fuck for money? I genuinely couldn't care less."

He relaxes a little more. "I know. I can tell. You...don't look at me any differently than you did before you saw me dance."

*Oh, I do. But not the way you think.*

"So, does that answer your question? About why I didn't grab your ass?"

Adrian gives a soft laugh, and he puts his hand over mine on his leg. "Yeah. It does." He pauses. "For the record, I didn't think you were like the other guys. Thinking I was a piece of meat. I just get a little more defensive about it than I should."

"If it were me, I'd probably be a lot more than a little defensive."

Another quiet laugh, but with a lot less feeling. Staring straight ahead, he takes in a breath. "The guy I was seeing... the dentist. He..." Adrian gnaws his lip. "It wasn't just that he didn't want people knowing he was with a stripper. He didn't want his *wife* to know."

I flinch. "Ouch."

"Yeah. I made the trip out to see him three times, and the last time, his wife came home from out of town a day early."

"She catch you guys?"

Adrian nods. "And while she was throwing a fit and threatening to destroy him in divorce court, he just kept telling her over and over that I was a hygienist he'd met in school. Like, he could get over being caught in their bed with a man, but admitting he was with a prostitute—one he wasn't even paying—was too much." He rolls his eyes. "I left and didn't look back, and couldn't give two shits how things played out with his wife. I was just pissed because that was the second time I'd found out I was someone's side piece."

"That's always brutal, isn't it?"

"You've had the pleasure?"

I groan.

"Really?"

"Yep. Before I met my ex, I had a thing going with a colleague who I'd see at conferences and whatnot. Thank God one of my coworkers caught on and kindly pointed out that he was married."

Adrian grimaces. "Anyone ever tell you not to fish off the company pier?"

I chuckle. "If I hadn't fished off that pier, I never would've done any fishing at all."

His expression turns serious. He's quiet long enough to overtake an eighteen wheeler that's going way too fucking slow, and then he asks, "So you really didn't have anyone outside of work?"

I shake my head. "Not when I lived and breathed my job, no. And no one ever told me that if the job went away, the people went with it."

"So you know what not to do the next time around."

It gives me pause to hear how he says that. How the next time around is a foregone conclusion for him. Like he just knows and accepts that I'm getting my shit together and I'm going to be okay. I wish I had his optimism.

But I just say, "Yeah. I do."

~*~

We reach Los Angeles during peak traffic. Of course, traffic is always hellish in this city, but certain times—like six o'clock on a Friday evening—are worse than others. I offer to switch and drive us through the worst of it, but Adrian handles it just fine. He's a pretty chill driver. Probably a result of not spending his formative years weaving through gridlock and trying to set other cars on fire with his mind. A traffic jam isn't nearly as stressful for someone who doesn't have years of road rage in his bone marrow.

There's a motel near LAX that's not one of the glitzy expensive places but also isn't one of the scary cheap ones in a bad neighborhood. We made a reservation last night through a travel site and got a decent deal on it. I try not to think about where I would've stayed if I'd been coming into town in my old life. Granted, I'd have been staying at my own fucking condo in West goddamned Hollywood instead of renting something out by the airport, but if I'd been a hypothetical tourist, I wouldn't have been staying at a no-name motel, and I sure as shit wouldn't have downgraded a king room to a queen to save thirteen dollars.

But here we are.

Adrian drops his bag on the floor at his feet and sprawls across the queen size bed. "Oh my God. I'm so glad to be out of the car."

I put my bag on the dresser beside the TV. "I thought you liked road trips."

"I do." He rubs his eyes with the heels of his hands. "But there's still nothing better than getting out of the car at the end of the day."

"Fair point." I ease myself down onto the bed beside him and drape an arm over his stomach. "Thank you again for driving. Riding shotgun with you was much more appealing than playing seatmate roulette on a Greyhound."

Adrian laughs, lowering his hands, and he rests them both on my arm. "Thanks for letting me tag along."

"Letting you? Please. You offered to help. I'm grateful as fuck, believe me."

"I know, but..." His smile turns a little shy. Then he slides closer, shifts onto his side, and puts his arm over my waist. "To be perfectly honest? I wanted to spend more time with you."

"Seriously?"

He nods, a faint blush blooming in his cheeks. "I do want to help. Really. But there might've been some selfishness in there too."

"I won't tell if you won't." I tip up his chin and press a soft kiss to his lips. "Especially since I'm really, really glad you're here."

He smiles, then pulls me in for another kiss. Neither of us is in any hurry to pull apart, so we don't. After a moment, I ease him onto his back, and we both sigh as my hips settle between his legs.

I lean down to kiss his neck, and he murmurs, "If we're going to do this, I should really grab a shower first."

"Mmm, a shower sounds like a good idea." I let my lips skim along the edge of his jaw. "Maybe I should join you."

"Maybe you should."

~*~

The storage unit door rolls up and clangs into place, echoing through the entire climate-controlled hallway.

Inside are boxes. Stacks and stacks of boxes. Most of them are labeled in black Sharpie—*textbooks*, *clothes-biz*, *DVDs*.

My stomach sinks a little at the sight. This is going to take fucking ages, and there's no guarantee any of it will bring in any money. Definitely no guarantee it'll be enough to put a dent in my situation.

Though, if memory serves, there are still some electronics in here. I did take the sixty-inch plasma screen out of the condo before the bank reclaimed the place, didn't I? And I'm pretty sure there's a set of my grandma's china in here somewhere that might be worth a little bit. Isn't like I'm ever going to use it.

"So." Adrian scans the boxes. "Where do we start?"

"At the front, I guess." I pull down one of the DVD boxes. "I don't imagine these will go very far. Even the Blu-Ray. But I guess it might be worth dragging them into a pawn shop."

He wrinkles his nose. "You'll get about a buck for the whole collection from a pawn shop. You're way better off putting them on eBay."

"Yeah, except a pawn shop will give me money today. eBay? That might be a week or two."

"So we'll take some other stuff to a pawn shop. But these? Definitely couldn't hurt to list them individually. Even if you get two or three bucks apiece, it's better than what a pawn shop would give you."

I give the box the side-eye.

"I have my laptop with me, and my phone takes decent photos," he says. "I could list them while you're at your interviews tomorrow."

My stomach tries to fold in on itself at the thought of those interviews, and I tamp down that particular breed of anxiety. "Okay. Sure. That could work." God, I'm going to owe him so big after all this is over.

Adrian drags the box out into the hall, sits cross-legged on the floor, and starts going through the DVDs, snapping a photo of each cover as he goes. While he does that, I pull down one of the boxes containing business clothes. Talk about a dodged bullet—during an especially low period, I'd almost donated these or just tossed them out on the curb. Somehow, enough optimism had crept in that I *might* need to go to a job interview, and I'd kept a few suits, ties, and dress shoes. I'd even had the foresight to keep it at the front of the storage unit just in case I needed to grab a suit on a moment's notice.

They're all folded neatly, and if I let them hang in the bathroom after I take a shower later, the steam will sort out any stray wrinkles. I think the room has an iron anyhow. If it doesn't, maybe housekeeping will let me borrow one.

I take the box down to Adrian's car and slide it into the backseat. When I come back, he's reading the blurb on one of the DVD cases.

"You have a lot of horror movies," he says without looking up.

"Just wait till you find the box with all the war movies. In fact, that might've even wound up being two boxes."

He lifts his gaze, and his eyes are lit up like a kid on Christmas. "Seriously?"

"Yeah. You into that kind of thing?"

"Hell yeah. I snuck into the theater three different times to watch *The Hedge*." He chuckles as he puts the DVD—*Carrie*, I can see now—onto the neat stack beside his hip. "The manager was pissed because she didn't want kids seeing that one."

I reach for a box but pause. "Wait, you were a kid when *The Hedge* came out?"

"Mmhmm." He glances up from pulling out my copy of *Last House on the Left*. "I was in sixth grade. So...twelve, I guess?"

I groan and turn to get that other box.

"Why?" The smirk is palpable in his voice. "How old were you?"

"When *The Hedge* came out?" I put the box down with a heavy thud. "I must've been..." I try to put my finger on where that movie was in my timeline, but finally settle on, "Okay, how old are you now?"

"Twenty-seven."

"Then I was twenty-four when it came out."

"So you're thirty-nine?"

"Mmhmm. Trust a blackjack dealer to be able to add that in a split second."

He just laughs. "You don't look it, by the way."

"Hmm?" I twist around, and he looks at me through his lashes before shifting his attention to photographing the cover of the DVD in his hand.

"You look younger." He puts the DVD aside and leans over to get another out. "I would've guessed you were… I don't know, early thirties, tops? After you said you'd been working in your field for sixteen years, I figured you weren't, but I wouldn't have guessed otherwise."

"Oh. So the gray doesn't give me away?"

"You don't have that much gray." He glances at me, then looks again and holds it a moment longer. "Nope." He shakes his head. "Not much."

"Well, at least I have something going for me." I open the next box and find some of my casual clothes. That's a hard thing to look at. I don't necessarily remember packing and labeling each box that's in this storage unit, but I distinctly remember this one. It's hard to forget a demoralizing moment like realizing you need to box up your everyday clothes because the only place you can keep them is your storage unit.

They gave me a deal on this unit, cutting me a huge discount if I paid for two years upfront. So I had because…why the hell not? I'd had no idea at the time that this would eventually be the only place on earth where I could keep any of my belongings. Or that there'd ever come a day when I'd need to come through those belongings so I might scrounge up enough cash to scrape by for a few weeks until a job came along.

"Max?"

I jump and turn around. "Hmm?"

He watches me, head cocked a little. "You kind of zoned out. You okay?"

"Yeah." I force a faint smile and then face the box again. "Lot of memories. That's all."

He doesn't press.

~*~

"So. How does it look?" I stand in front of the foot of the bed and spread my arms, modeling the navy blue suit.

Adrian's leaning against the headboard with his laptop on his knees, and he looks at me over the screen. A grin spreads across his lips that makes my heart race. "I like it." With a wink, he adds, "Shame you don't want it getting wrinkled."

I don't even try to hide the shiver, and he knows it.

Still grinning, he gets back to work.

*Clickety-clickety-clickety.*

His hands are flying across the keyboard. He's been listing my DVDs on eBay for the past hour, and he's found his groove—he's *fast*.

While he's doing that, I've gone through the box of business clothes and pulled together a suit for my interview tomorrow. I also found a blue tie to go with it, and I weave around all the other boxes—the half dozen or so we hauled back with us—to the bathroom.

Though my days of wearing shirts and ties feel like eons ago, the muscle memory is still there. I quickly put on the tie, slide the knot to my throat, and adjust the collar. Then I tug at my sleeves, brush off my lapels, and button the coat.

Apparently I've lost some weight since the last time I put this thing on. Not just from being on the street, either. The waistband on the trousers is loose, and the jacket doesn't sit *quite* right. Nothing a belt can't help in the short term and a tailor can't fix in the long run, but it feels odd.

This is a suit I used to wear like a second skin. And now it doesn't feel right.

I look myself up and down in the mirror. When I meet my own eyes, the tie seems to be getting tighter even though my hands aren't on it. I tug at the knot, but the air still seems thicker than it should be.

Heart thumping, I rest my hands on the counter's cool edge and hold my own gaze.

*I don't know who I am anymore.*

I'm looking at a man I saw every morning and every evening for sixteen years. Suit and tie and confidence. That guy's not quite right against the background of a butterscotch-colored shower curtain and the chipped mint green tile wall under stark fluorescent lights, but he's me.

He *was* me.

The last time I saw this face was in a hotel bathroom of an entirely different caliber. I was in my gray suit that night, still not entirely sure why I needed to be found dressed like that, but unconsciously insistent that it was the right way to look. When I'd looked at myself, I'd seen this guy—the advertising executive who'd lost his way and would leave precisely nothing behind except a hard drive full of ad campaigns and travel invoices at a firm who'd probably already forgotten his name.

I swallow, my throat pushing against the loosened tie. I swear I can taste the bitterness of the pills, and at the same time, the sour acid after I'd heaved them up.

The moment between swallowing the pills and throwing them back up isn't one I've thought about until now. It's not that I've forgotten it. Blocked it out, maybe. Ignored it. Pretended it was a dream or something I saw in a movie.

But no, it was real.

I took the pills too fast, and one stuck itself to the back of my throat. The bitterness and the burn were too unpleasant to ignore, even though I knew it would be over soon, and I went into the bathroom for some more water to wash it down.

One gulp of water dislodged the stupid pill.

Then I looked at myself like I'm doing now.

And I froze.

This was all that would be left of me. A suited and booted failure who couldn't even say "*I lost my job, but at least I...*" because there was nothing to finish that sentence. At least I, what? Fucked a few guys who were distant memories now? Accumulated a bunch of crap that would all be auctioned off because I didn't have *one single person* to leave anything to in the will I never got around to writing anyway?

In the space of seconds, my determination to see things through didn't go away. Instead, it was eclipsed by the fierce and terrified need to throw the freight train into reverse.

I'd spun, dropped to my knees, and jammed my fingers down my throat until I was absolutely sure my stomach had nothing left to throw up.

In the present, my knees start shaking. The memory is so visceral, I steal a glance toward the toilet to make absolutely sure I know how far I need to go to if I suddenly need to puke. I grip the counter's edge, which is warm and damp from my hands.

Less than two weeks ago, I had, for all intents and purposes, pulled the trigger.

*I should be dead.*

My reflection blurs. I swipe at my eyes, too overwhelmed by too many emotions to give even one of them a name. It's that feeling like I've nearly been in a catastrophic car crash and missed disaster by the skin of my teeth. That shaky, dizzy, queasy feeling of my heart pounding faster than it should be able to as I nose off the road and try to take stock of what happened and how in the world I survived. A million emotions, all at once, heightened by the disbelief that I'm alive to experience them.

"Hey, do you know if you have the first volume of—" Adrian stops speaking the instant he appears in the doorway, a DVD in hand. His gaze is locked on me. "You okay?"

"Yeah." I wipe my eyes again, not that it helps. And my hand is shaking, and I'm so obviously not okay, but I silently plead with him to take my word for it.

He sets the DVD on the counter and slips an arm around me. Without really thinking, I put mine around his shoulders, and he just fits so perfectly against me. Once we're settled into a gentle, foundation-rattling embrace, he asks, "What's wrong?"

I squeeze my eyes shut, and the warm trickle down my cheek has got to be a dead giveaway. Still, I try to tell myself he might not have seen it.

No such luck—he gently wipes it away.

I catch his wrist and press a kiss to his palm. His fingers relax into a caress, and even after I let go, he keeps his hand there.

Finally, I open my eyes and look at us in the mirror. "I was just thinking. About what I almost did in Vegas."

He tenses so subtly, I wouldn't have noticed if he weren't fitted against me like this. "Killing yourself, you mean?"

It's my turn to tense. "Yeah." I swallow the lump in my throat and hold Adrian close to my chest. "It's just…kind of terrifying to think how close I came to going through with it."

He holds on a little tighter too. For a while, neither of us speaks. He doesn't ask for gory details or explanations. He's just here, as if—for the second time—he knows I need him right now.

Eventually, he whispers, "I'm not sure how much it helps, but…I'm really glad you didn't."

I press a kiss to his forehead. "Me too."

Adrian lifts his chin, and our eyes meet. I brush a few strands of black hair out of his face so I can see his beautiful blue eyes. He's not wearing makeup this time, but the blue is still vivid as ever.

*I don't think you will ever understand how close I came to missing this.*

And I don't want to break down and lose it. Not now. He's here, gazing up at me like there's nowhere else in the world he wants to be, and there's nowhere else I want to be either. I'm just grateful beyond belief that I'm here at all.

So I slide my hand into his hair and kiss him.

Adrian melts against me, lips parting so one of us— I'm not even sure who—can deepen the kiss. He doesn't taste bitter or sour. He just tastes like *him*. There's a hint of citrus from the Mountain Dew he was drinking earlier, but even that is unmistakably Adrian because I was there when he was drinking it. I never liked that stuff, but damn if I'm not getting high off it this time because *Adrian*.

He breaks the kiss and cradles my face. Apparently another tear got loose, and he wipes it away before he presses another kiss—soft, tender, and brief—to my lips.

When our eyes meet again, he says, "Seeing you like this doesn't turn me on or anything, but…" He swallows. "I kind of want to take you into the other room. Like now." The sudden intensity in his eyes brings goose bumps to life all over me.

"Why's that?"

He strokes my cheek with the pad of his thumb. "So we can fuck until you understand how much I want you to stay alive."

# Chapter 13
## Adrian

Fully-dressed, Max sinks onto the hard bed on his back, and I land gently on top of him. His coat's unbuttoned and his tie is undone, but otherwise, we're not getting very far with getting clothes out of the way.

Fine. I'm in no hurry. Seeing Max like that in the bathroom shook something in me, and I need to have him until it's settled back down again.

*I've only known you a week,* I want to tell him. *I don't know why I care this much, but I do.*

I just can't figure out how to say that without sounding insane. The physical side, though? Letting him know how much I want him? That I can do. In spades.

His fingers comb through my hair as his tongue explores my mouth like this is the first time we've ever kissed. When I start unbuttoning his shirt, he moans softly and makes an attempt to untuck my T-shirt from my shorts before his hand gets distracted and comes to rest on my ass. I keep rubbing my clothed cock and balls against him, turning myself inside out at the same time I'm making him moan and tremble. I don't even know how I want this to play out. If I want him to fuck me like he did the first night, or if I want to top him this time. Or if I just want us to make out and touch each other until we both come. I don't know, and I don't really care as long as Max keeps gasping and shaking and cursing between kisses.

His hands move again, and this time, he gets my shirt completely untucked, and pushes it up and off. As his palms slide down my chest, my body responds as if no man has ever made contact with my naked skin. I shiver, which makes me press even harder against him, and now I'm desperate for… not an orgasm, but something that might lead to one. I need my dick in his hand, or his mouth, or his ass. *Something.*

"I want you naked," I blurt out between kisses.

He groans, kneading my ass with both hands. "Yeah. Naked." Fuck, the hunger in his voice turns me on like crazy.

Somehow, clothes start coming off. We're still making out, still rubbing and grinding, but belts come open and flies are unzipped and his jacket winds up on the floor. More and more skin touches skin. When he drags his nails down my thighs, he scrapes bare flesh and leaves behind stripes of pure heat that do nothing to quell this growing need to fucking *come.*

God only knows how, but we kick off everything else. Then Max wraps his arms around me and rolls me onto my back, and I damn near cry as his hips come down between my parted thighs. I can't get enough of him. His body, his kiss, the heat radiating off his skin.

In a small way—as much as it'll ever be possible, I think—I get why he was so emotional in the bathroom. As we hold on and wind each other up, I'm jarringly aware of how close I came to never knowing him at all beyond a few hands of cards at my blackjack table. It's one thing to be ships passing in the night. It's another to imagine that other ship sinking to the bottom while mine sails on without ever knowing there was any distress.

If realizing that rocks my foundation this much, then I definitely understand why it hit him so hard. I just hope like hell it hit him hard enough to keep him from going to that place again.

That thought makes me hold him even tighter and kiss him even more hungrily. I've never needed someone like this before. Not just for my own release, or because I want to make him feel good, but because I want him to be okay. I want to reassure myself he's really alive, and I want him to *feel* that alive.

I slide a hand between us and close it around his cock. He groans against my lips, rocking gently into my fist, and every time the head of his cock pushes past my fingers, my head spins faster at the memory of him riding me. Usually I'm completely vers with a guy, and I get bored with guys who are strictly a top or bottom, but with Max, I just want to take his cock over and over and over until I can still feel him next week, and then I want to do it again.

He breaks the kiss and starts down my neck. I tilt my head back into the pillow, annoyed for a split second that it's too firm for me to go very far, but Max does just fine with what I offer up. His five o'clock shadow burns alongside the tickle of his lips, and when he lets his teeth graze my skin, I curse loud enough I probably startle the people in the next room.

Max laughs softly and does it again. "Like that, don't you?"

"Uh-huh." I tighten my grasp on his cock, and he growls against the side of my throat. "Condoms are...in your bag, right?"

"Mmhmm." He makes no move to reach for it. Instead, he keeps kissing up my neck, all the way my jaw, and starts back down again.

I'm so turned on and needy right now, especially since I've made up my mind and want him balls deep in me, but I can't make him stop what he's doing. "*Fuck*, I love that."

He grins against my skin. "I know you do." He bites me again, and when I gasp, his cock stiffens in my hand. I stroke him a little harder, and now he's the one getting all flustered and vocal. Neither of us lets up, either. The more he kisses and nibbles my neck, the more I stroke and tease his dick, and in no time flat, we're both out of breath and squirming.

Finally, he pushes himself up. "I'm getting a condom."

I just moan.

When he comes back, he pauses. "So who's—"

"You put it on," I say between gulps of air. "And get on your back."

His eyes widen a little, and I think he shivers. He doesn't protest, though, and he gets on his back next to me. While he deals with the condom, I pour some lube in my hand. I love the way his hands are shaking now. He can barely get the wrapper open. As he rolls the condom onto his cock, his back arches like even that's too much stimulation to ignore. Between that and the flush of his neck and chest, he's so unavoidably aroused, I can barely stand it.

"There," he says as he lifts his hands away. "Now get on." It's less of a command and more of a *please do it now before I explode*, and I love it.

I stroke the lube onto the condom. Max closes his eyes, biting his lip as he pushes his hips up and fucks into my hand again. Teasing him is tempting, but damn it, I need that cock in me right now before *I'm* the one who explodes.

I straddle him, and he steadies his cock while I guide myself down. Oh fuck, just the head pressing against my hole sends electricity right through me. I push back a little and ease myself onto him, and when the head slips in, I'm surprise I *don't* come.

"Fuck," I breathe. The first time we did this, he'd spent ages rimming me until I was so relaxed, I probably could've taken the whole thing all at once. This time, the penetration burns a little more. Stretches more. And dear God, it feels good.

I lift off him again and come back down so I can have that first inch all over again. I love the way it feels. Something about that initial invasiveness, going from wanting it to having it, is addictive.

"Holy fuck," he moans. His hands are on my thighs now, and the way his muscles are quivering, I wonder if he's trying not to thrust up into me. I can't decide if I want him to stay still and let me be in control or if I want him to grab me, pull me down onto him, and force himself as deep as I can take him. It's like reaching the decision page in a *Choose Your Own Adventure*, and not being able to choose which way to turn. Except I don't remember any of those weathered old paperbacks having options like these.

A laugh escapes my lips. Wow, I am *deliriously* turned on right now.

I ease myself down, taking more of him. As I do, I can't take my eyes off his face. He's flushed, his brow pinched and his lips apart as he watches his cock slide deeper into me. I love the way his abs quiver and his jaw works as he visibly tries to stay in control. We've only fucked a couple of times, but I know how hard and rough he can give it to me, and I know what he looks and sounds like when he lets go and loses it. The thought of him taking over, throwing me on my back, and pounding me into oblivion is hot, but the sight of him reining it in, letting me be in control, and *just* restraining himself is *unbelievably* hot.

Squeezing his eyes shut, he arches his back and grips my thighs even tighter. "Oh God…"

I take more of him. *All* of him. My ass is pressed against his hips, and he's buried to the hilt in me, and it's so, so tempting to ride him hard and fast until this need for release is finally satisfied, but I don't want this to be over yet. I'm on that edge between desperately needing to do whatever it takes to get myself off and still being able to hold back enough to draw this out, and though I'm too far gone to think about why, I'm aware my time with him is limited. My body wants the shortest distance between here and shooting cum all over Max's chest, but the rest of me needs to take the scenic route.

I lean forward and brush my lips across his. Without a second's hesitation, he's got his arms around me, and he's kissing me full-on, and…this is perfect. Oh my God. He's out of breath, and hot huffs of air rush past my cheek as he slides his tongue alongside mine.

We're moving together somehow—I don't know who's leading and who's following, or even whose idea it was, only that his cock is sliding in and out, and skin is brushing skin, and I can't get enough.

A shudder jolts him hard enough to break the kiss. He sinks back onto the bed—I can't remember when he levitated off it, but apparently he did—and pushes up into me. "Jesus, Adrian…" He licks his lips. "Oh my God…"

"You feel so good," I whisper, breathing hard as I keep slowly riding his cock.

"So… So do you." He blinks a few times, then looks in my eyes. He's reaching for me again, and in my mind's eye, we're back to what we were doing a second ago—holding on and making out while we fuck.

But he doesn't pull me down.

He touches my face.

Just like he did at the strip club.

At the first brush of his fingertips on my cheek, my whole body breaks out in goose bumps. I've never been with a man like him. One who can be so turned on that any man would only be thinking of whatever it takes to get himself off, and he still touches…me.

"*When I asked to touch you,*" his words echo in my ears, "*it wasn't because I had a gorgeous piece of ass in my lap and wanted to cop a few feels and maybe fuck. It was because I wanted* you."

My heart's going crazy, and it's not all exertion.

*Now I want you. More than I probably should.*

I lean down again, and before our lips even meet, his hand is in my hair. We're kissing even more hungrily. More greedily. The bed creaks and my muscles ache and his cock is slamming into me, so we must be moving too, but I can't keep track of everything now. Only how utterly amazing I feel as we fuck and kiss and breathe and touch.

His skin is slick with sweat. So's mine. We're both breathing so hard we can barely kiss. My head is light, and my orgasm is so close I don't think I could stop it if I wanted to, and then he moans against my lips like he's about to burst out either laughing or crying, and his next thrust hits just right, and—

"Oh fuck!" I throw my head back. Rhythm is a distant memory, and all I can think is to keep moving so this feeling doesn't stop. Max grabs my hips and fucks me hard from below, and then he's got me in a death grip, holding me against him so he's as deep as I can take him, and though he doesn't make a sound, I swear to God the shockwave from his orgasm is almost visible.

Someone shudders again—I don't know who—and we both exhale. I sink down into his arms, head falling beside his. I don't give a damn about the cum that's all over his—and now my—stomach. I close my eyes and just lie there for a moment, feeling both of our hearts pounding as his chest rises and falls under me.

"I don't even smoke," he slurs, "but I could almost go for a cigarette right now."

I laugh. "Yeah. Same."

He nudges me gently until I lift my head. When I do, he presses the most tender kiss to my lips.

Our eyes meet. His have a hint of tears in them, but I'm pretty sure they're not there for the same reason as they were in the bathroom. If he came half as hard as I did, then damn right his eyes are welling up.

He brushes a few strands of hair out of my face and tucks them behind my ear. "Any time you want to fuck like that? You just say the word."

I grin. "Likewise."

We both laugh kind of drunkenly, but as we hold each other's gazes, the humor fades and the rest of the world sets in. The reasons we ended up like this in the first place—both why we met on the street in front of the Bellagio, and why we're tangled up in this motel bed with his cock still inside me. How easily none of this could have happened.

I come back down and kiss him. "I am so glad," I pant against his lips, "that you're still here."

"Yeah." He combs his fingers through my hair. "Me too."

# Chapter 14
## Max

I still can't quite piece together how I went from staring myself down in the bathroom to tangled up with Adrian in the hard queen-size bed.

The chain of events is clear enough. It's not that I don't *remember* anything. It's just hard to comprehend *how* it happened. How Adrian wasn't put off by my mini breakdown and in fact had dragged me to bed.

*"Seeing you like this doesn't turn me on or anything, but I kind of want to take you into the other room. Like now."*

*"Why's that?"*

*"So we can fuck until you understand how much I want you to stay alive."*

Nothing about it felt like a pity fuck. Or like he just wanted to have sex so I'd forget about my depressing crap and stop being such a downer. I don't know that I've ever been in bed with someone who seemed that eager to be there with *me*.

He's dozing on my shoulder now. Some of his long hair has tumbled down, and it's cool against my skin. His breath is soft, warm, and steady.

As relaxed as he is, I can't help noticing that the arm he's got draped over me isn't exactly a wet noodle. There's some strength there. Some tension. Like he's holding on.

I press my lips to his forehead. *I'm not going anywhere, Adrian.*

Except that isn't entirely true. I'm in no rush to get out of this bed, and I'm certainly in no hurry for us to go back to living our lives in separate cities. I hope we'll stay in contact, of course, but this is a finite thing. The sex is fun, but I can't imagine he's really onboard with saddling himself with someone who's just starting to scrape himself up off rock bottom. The novelty of fucking at every opportunity wears thin real quick when you're dating a loser.

So I'm in no rush to leave, but I also don't have any illusions that this thing has legs. He'll stay with me for a few days while I get my shit together, and we'll probably have some spectacular goodbye sex right before he leaves, and that'll be it.

*But you're here tonight. Thank God, you're here tonight.*

He stirs a little, and his arm loosens. "Shit, did I fall asleep?"

"Probably." I trail my fingers up and down his other arm. "It's okay."

He rubs his face as he lifts himself up onto his elbow. "How long was I out?"

"Eh." I shrug. "A few minutes, maybe?"

"Damn. Sorry about that."

"Don't worry about it. I was comfortable, and you seemed to be too." With a grin, I add, "Plus it just means I wore you out. Mission accomplished."

Adrian laughs. He cranes his neck a little to kiss me. "I might get a second wind, though. So, you know—be ready to wear me out again."

"I'm pretty sure I can do that."

We both laugh. He rests in his hand in the middle of my chest, and under the covers, his foot slides over my shin. With some guys in the past, this kind of thing has felt clingy, but it doesn't with him. It's actually really nice. I like being next to someone who wants to touch me when we're not actually fooling around.

It's mutual, too. In fact, it's hard to keep my hands off him. He doesn't seem to mind either, though. Whenever I brush his hair back, he presses against my hand like a cat. In bed, when I've got my arm around him, he cuddles closer. I could really get used to this, and I probably will even though I know I shouldn't.

I run the backs of my fingers along the smooth edge of his jaw. "I'm, uh, sorry about earlier. In the bathroom."

"Sorry?" He cocks his head. "Why?"

"I…guess I was…" Well shit. Now I feel like an idiot.

Adrian slides a hand up onto my shoulder and rests it there. "With everything that's happened recently, I'm not surprised. To be honest, I'm amazed that anyone could get that low and still pull themselves back up."

Heat rushes into my cheeks. "Let's not put the cart before the horse here. I haven't pulled myself up *yet*."

"Compared to when I found you on the street? Or when you almost took the pills?"

I swallow. I can't bring myself to tell him there was no "almost" about it. But he does have a point. "I hadn't looked at it that way."

He's watching me now. Intently. I've gotten used to that look—where he's trying to read me but doesn't seem like he's judging me or silently shaming me. After a moment, he says, "Are you going to be okay? I mean, between now and when you're really back on your feet?"

"I think so. I'm… It wasn't like I was prone to depression or anything before this. One of my colleagues was. He had to take meds and see a therapist a couple of times a week, and even then, he'd go through suicidal phases sometimes. I don't think this is that kind of thing. I just had my whole life pulled out from under me, and kind of…caved in, I guess."

"So you've never been suicidal before?"

I shake my head. "No. Never. And I don't…" I stare up at the ceiling as I try to gather my thoughts. "I don't think I ever actually wanted to die."

"What do you mean?"

It takes a moment to pull the right words from my brain. "I mean, I felt more like I was already dead. My life literally seemed like it was over, and I guess I was just…finishing the job." I close my eyes and sigh. "It wasn't until I was standing on the metaphorical ledge that I realized just how much I *didn't* want to die. And I still don't. I'm not sure how the future is going to play out, but dying is…" I shake my head before I turn to him again. "I think it's safe to say I got close enough to the edge to know I have no desire to go back."

His brow pinches and he gnaws his lip. He doesn't look convinced.

"I'm serious." I smooth his hair. I love how it feels between my fingers. "I'm not going back to that."

"I believe you, but…" He searches my eyes. "Can I… I guess it's not really my place to ask you to promise anything."

"Try me."

Adrian swallows. "Will you at least talk to someone? Like a therapist?"

I hadn't thought about it, and if anyone had suggested it to me before, I probably would've told them to fuck off. Now that he's put it out there, though, it really doesn't seem like such a bad idea. I don't see how I could ever go back to that dark place. On the other hand, I never saw myself going there to begin with, and look at me now.

"Okay." I trace his cheekbone with the pad of my thumb. "When I've got health insurance or something, I'll look into it."

That eases some of the tension in his expression, and he smiles. "Okay. I just, you know, want you to be all right."

I smile back. "I will be."

And little by little, I was starting to believe it.

~*~

Adrian has all the DVDs listed on eBay by the end of the night, and the next morning, we go back to the storage unit continue sifting through what's left of my belongings.

By mid-afternoon, he's photographed the things we think will pull in some decent money. Mostly furniture—the mahogany sleigh bed I had for six months before everything went to shit. The gorgeous hardwood dining room set that used to look spectacular in my sunny condo. A hallway table with a marble top and hand-carved legs.

It's a relief to have this much that can potentially bring in money, but it's kind of depressing too. Mostly because I pulled out the occasional thing that I can't part with for sentimental reasons, and that amounts to...very little. A shoebox of photos, plus two albums. My framed degrees. A mix CD I've had since high school—it's a memorial a friend put together after one of our other friends was killed in a car accident. Aside from a few other odds and ends, that's pretty much it. Everything worth carrying from my past life fits into a single box that used to be full of mismatched Tupperware.

Back in our motel room, the mountain of boxes is huge, but it's mostly smaller things we're listing on eBay and craigslist. Adrian's ridiculously efficient at this, and he types so fast his fingers blur over the keyboard of the laptop he's balancing on his knee.

*Clickety-clickety-clickety.*

I'm not quite as fast as he is, but I'm making progress. I found my laptop in the mix this morning, and after it went through a few thousand updates, it's connected to the Wi-Fi so I can put up some listings too. And respond to messages we've already gotten about a few things.

Somebody went through and clicked Buy It Now on a dozen DVD listings, so that's almost a hundred bucks I didn't have before. I have some old vinyl albums that are apparently worth something too—there's a bidding war going on one of them, and the others have some nibbles too.

As we list the furniture and everything else, my gaze keeps drifting toward the stack of boxes we've kept aside from all the rest. This stack is much smaller—just a medium sized cardboard box with NOT FOR SALE scrawled on the side and an old wooden one about the size of a tackle box sitting on top.

Inside the cardboard one are the photos and other things I couldn't part with.

It's the wooden box that keeps pulling my attention, though. That came from my mother. Inside are some letters and postcards I still can't make myself read and a few pieces of jewelry she inherited from my grandmother.

It's kind of ironic that in the end, all she really had left was that little box of mementos and keepsakes. Like me, she had to sell off most of what she owned in a desperate bid to survive. The difference was she was trying to pay for cancer treatment.

I absently run my thumb along the edge of the laptop I'm balancing on my leg and stare at that box. To this day, I wish I'd been paying closer attention to my mom's deterioration. As with everything in my life, I'd been too swallowed up by work to be anything but oblivious. And as she'd always been, Mom was too stubborn and proud to ask for help while that help might've actually made a difference.

I'd known she was sick. Of course I had. I just hadn't realized *how* sick, or how little her insurance had been covering. I'll never know if I could have contributed enough to pay for treatment that might've really helped or if the cancer was just too aggressive, but at least she could have focused on her health instead of selling everything she owned and sweating over the bills she still couldn't pay. As it was, I didn't find out how bad things really were until I went home for Christmas and realized she didn't even have heat.

By then, there wasn't much the doctors could do. It's cold comfort knowing that at least I was able to help her get enough pain medication to make her last few weeks more bearable.

And in the end, she was gone, and all she left behind was that little wooden box and about twenty thousand dollars of debt.

There's a lesson to be learned in there, I'm sure. Something about not waiting until shit's out of control before asking for help. Maybe. I don't know. My mother's gone, a handful of her things are still here, and by the time the dust settles, I won't have many more of my own possessions left.

It's not that I'm materialistic. I'm okay with not having a ton of things. It's just weird to imagine dying and leaving nothing behind. Not having anything that a person can take with them to remember me by. Like that CD from when my friend was killed. I've never forgotten her, but something about the CD makes her feel a little less gone. Like there's a tangible thing to reassure me that she really was here. Touching it and looking at the photo on the cover makes her memory more vivid. Even now, twenty years later, hearing one of the songs still makes my breath catch.

I don't need some big fancy grave marker when I die—I'll probably ask for my ashes to be scattered somewhere just like my mother did. I just hope there's someone, somewhere who might touch something or hear a song and remember I was here at all.

"Hey." Adrian nudges me. "You timed out."

"Huh?" I look at the screen. Sure enough, the ad I was writing has disappeared, replaced by a login screen. How long was I staring into space?

"You okay?"

"Yeah." I shake myself and log back in. "I'm good."

He watches me for a moment, and I'm almost certain he's going to ask me to explain it.

He doesn't, though. He just goes back to listing the bed frame on craigslist.

*Clickety-clickety-clickety.*

# Chapter 15
## Adrian

The responses to our ads come in quickly and in droves. The bed frame is sold before we even take a break for dinner. By the time we go to bed, he's had half a dozen inquiries about the dining room set, and when we pause between fucking and going to sleep, the dining room set and the marble table are sold.

While Max is at his job interviews the next day, I drive back to the storage unit to meet the buyers for the bigger pieces. The tables and chairs are gone by ten, but of course, the couple coming to get the bed are delayed. Fortunately, there's a diner across the street, so I text them and let them know I'll wait for them there.

As I walk into the place, I suppress a snicker. I'm used to cheesy places that try way too hard. That's basically the definition of Las Vegas. If it should be tall, make it taller. If it should be loud, make it louder. If it needs a couple of lights, cover it in thousands of them and make sure they blink and are visible from space.

And even I'm a little taken aback by this place.

The restaurant is probably the size of your average Denny's. In fact, I think it *was* a Denny's in a past life. I have no idea how they fit this much chrome inside one building, but there it is, gleaming on every surface. The staff must tear their hair out trying to keep it clean—I swear I left fingerprints on the hostess stand just by looking at it from five feet away.

The wait staff and cooks are all dressed like they just walked out of a bad 1950s movie. Short skirts. Paper hats. The works. Lucky this isn't a drive-in or they'd probably have to wear roller skates.

It's cheesy and ridiculous but kind of charming too, and the sizzle of burgers on a grill makes my mouth water. I'm going to need to find a gym around here where I can do a "trial membership" if I want to fit into my clothes when I go home. Especially when it's time to dance.

Then again, I've been doing plenty of cardio with Max, so I decide that's enough and don't feel the least bit guilty ordering a deluxe bacon cheeseburger with cheese-smothered fries.

While I wait for the food, I gaze out the window. There isn't much to see from here. The three-story storage facility, of course. A gas station. Some fast food place I've never heard of. In the distance, the hazy outline of some mountains tells me I'm facing east. More or less looking at Vegas, now that I think about it.

It's going to be weird to go back. I've lived there my whole life, and going home has always felt like…going home. I'm sure it will this time too. My house, my jobs, my friends, my fish—they're all there. Some family too, though Mom and Dad moved to Phoenix and my brother is in some town I can't pronounce in Pennsylvania. But it's basically home. Even when I go visit my parents, I never feel weird when I leave to come back to Vegas. I miss them, and I wish we all lived closer, but there's never that feeling that I'm leaving for the last time.

Ah. That's it. When I drive out of Los Angeles, I have no idea if I'll be coming back. Or if I do, I don't know if it'll be to see Max.

I'm not quite as hungry all of a sudden. I debate canceling my order, but I do need to eat. Max has enough to worry about, and he doesn't need to deal with a hangry Adrian.

Still, my stomach's all wound up in knots now. I'm being stupid and I know it. Max is getting his life back on track. I'm just here to help out with some of the nuts and bolts. And yeah, I'm here for some more of that amazing sex. This is temporary, though.

I've been on this mental wheel since last night, and no matter how much I rationalize and try to tell myself I just want to help him, the fact is, I want him. If we lived in the same city, I would absolutely want to date him. Not that I have high hopes about it being mutual. When he's down on his luck and homeless, yeah, he can probably cope with a stripper for a fuck buddy. Once he's on his way back to respectable...

My stomach knots even tighter.

Of course the waitress picks that exact moment to bring my lunch. And dear God, that is an awesome-looking bacon cheeseburger. It isn't one of those unnaturally perfect round patties, either. It's got all the rough edges of one that was made by hand. The fries? Steak fries. Dripping in melted cheddar, not some of that liquid crap. Oh fuck yes.

Though my gut is still angsting over Max, it doesn't object to a bite of hot, greasy burger with exactly the perfect amount of ketchup, mustard, pickles, and cheese. I take back everything I said about this place trying too hard. Their décor is over the top, but their food redeems every molecule of chrome.

While I eat, I try to be a little more objective about the way things are with Max.

I'm kidding myself if I think there's a future here. We come from two very different worlds, and not just because we're on opposite sides of the Sierra Nevada. He has degrees and colleagues and potential for promotions. I deal cards and take off my clothes for a living. He'll probably get bonuses and a company car. I get tips and propositions.

Would he really want to tell people about me? It's not just because I'm a sex worker or a lowly card dealer. Max has his pride. I can't imagine he'll get all that nostalgic about telling the story of how we met, since it means mentioning the part where I found him on the street with a cardboard sign.

I sigh as I drag a fry through some ketchup that dripped off my burger. Whether I like it or not, I'm part of a period in Max's life that I'm guessing he isn't going to want to brag about. Once he has a job and a place, he'll be smart to do everything he can to put this all behind him. Including me. The sooner I make peace with that, the easier it'll be to get in the car, point it toward Vegas, and go back to my own life when this is over.

In the meantime, I'll help him as much as I can. And I'll enjoy the time I do get to spend with him.

And hey—at least this burger tastes good.

~*~

I'm at the hotel when Max gets back. From the way he's smiling as he lets himself in, the interviews must have gone well.

I close my laptop and set it on the nightstand. "So? How did it go?"

"I'm not sure about the first one." He loosens his tie as he toes off his shoes. "The second one seems promising, though. It's someone I've worked with before, so at least she knows I'm not a complete fuck-up."

"That *is* promising." I swing my legs over the side of the bed. "What happens next?"

He shrugs off his coat and drapes it over the chair by the TV. "Now... I wait. If someone wants a second interview, they'll call." He pauses. "You, um, don't mind that I gave them your cell, do you?"

"No, of course not. I mean, it won't do them much good after I go back to Vegas, but if someone calls after I leave, I'll let you know."

Max smiles. He hooks his fingers in my belt loops and tugs me closer to him. "Thank you. I really appreciate it."

"I know." I lift my chin and kiss him lightly. Then I reach into my pocket and take out my wallet. "By the way, here's the cash for the furniture." I hand him the wad of bills. "Almost two grand, all told."

He stares at the money. "Whoa." Then he laughs and shakes his head as he takes out his wallet. "You know, a year ago, I wouldn't have thought twice about dropping two grand on a TV or a custom suit. Now?" He slides the money into his weathered billfold. "Feels like I hit the lottery."

"I can't even imagine."

"You don't want to. Trust me." He pauses, then clears his throat. "Anyway. I should check on the eBay auctions. See if anything else is—"

"There were a few more Buy It Nows earlier. There's about two hundred in your PayPal account." I swear, as soon as I say the words, his eyes almost start to well up. I touch his arm. "Looks like you're on your way to back on your feet."

"Yeah. Little by little." He smiles. "If I get one of these jobs, then all of this should be enough to tide me over until the first paycheck comes through." His eyes lose focus for a few long seconds, but his brow is creased like he's deep in thought, so I don't say anything. Finally, he sighs, rubbing his hand over his face. "My God. I might actually get my shit together."

"Well, my fingers are crossed for one of the jobs."

"Mine too." He puts a hand on my waist and gently draws me in. "You know, when I decided not to get on the bus out of Vegas and came to find you, it was because I wanted to buy you dinner. I still haven't done that."

"It's okay. You should probably hold on to whatever you have until things level out."

He tucks my hair behind my ear. "I should, yeah. But I think I can spare enough to take you out. After everything you've done, it's the least I can do."

I've long since accepted that he's hell bent on paying me back, so I know better than to fight it. "Okay. But nothing crazy, all right?" I realize a second too late that might not be the thing his wounded pride needs to hear, so I add, "All I brought are jeans and T-shirts. So nothing that requires a coat."

Max laughs, and there's a hint of relief. I think he knows exactly why I backpedaled. He presses a kiss to my forehead. "I think I know a place you'll like."

~*~

I balk as soon as I see the restaurant. There's no way this is within his budget, and we're both definitely underdressed for it. It's got that high-class exterior with the awnings over the windows and the fancy gold lettering above the doors. The kind of place that would let anyone in off the street in Vegas but probably not here in Los Angeles.

And the kind of place where everything costs a damn fortune.

"Max." I shake my head as we walk from the car up the block. "That place is way too—"

"Trust me." He puts his hand on the small of my back for just a second. "It's not as high-brow as it looks."

I shoot him a glance, still not convinced.

We stop outside the door, and there's a menu behind glass so passersby can peruse it before committing to a seat. It's a mix of European cuisines—mostly Mediterranean with a smattering of French and even a couple of German dishes—and the descriptions sound amazing. To my surprise, the prices aren't too bad either. Maybe more than I'd spend if I were in Max's situation, but we're not going to put him out on the street again if we order dessert. And judging by the couple in shorts and T-shirts who brush past us, the dress code is pretty lenient too.

"Okay." I try and fail to suppress a smile. "We'll give it a try."

"I thought you might see things my way." He gestures for me to go in ahead of him, and we step into a lobby that's filled with the rich scents of garlic and at least half a dozen herbs I can't name. One whiff, and I decide *I'll* pay if need be, but we are absolutely eating here.

The hostess shows us to a table for two. Despite how inexpensive and obviously relaxed this place is, it certainly doesn't look the part. The tablecloths are white linen, and little tea lights flicker next to the salt and pepper shakers. The menus are bound in what I assume is fake leather, but they don't look cheap or chintzy.

There's a large wine list on the table and a pair of wineglasses next to each place setting. It occurs to me now that we never discussed if dinner included wine. Inexpensive or not, I really don't want to add the price of a bottle or even a glass to the bill if he's paying it. So I don't touch the wine list. Neither does he.

Our waiter comes and takes our order. Max gets the shrimp fettuccini, and I get the carbonara. We both order iced teas. The waiter leaves with our menus and the wine list, and I'm admittedly relieved that no one mentions wine.

"I'm guessing you know this place?" I ask once we're alone.

Max nods. "Used to come here whenever I was in this part of town. I don't know how they stay in business when it's so expensive in this city, but they've been here for years."

My stomach knots suddenly. "This is an expensive city, isn't it?"

"God, yeah. It's brutal."

I'm not sure what to say. There's a question on the tip of my tongue, but I really don't want to kill the mood. Or, well…more than I've already killed it just by thinking of the stupid question.

"Adrian?" Max folds his forearms on the edge of the table. "You got quiet all of a sudden."

"Yeah, I…" *Fuck.*

Right then, the waiter materializes with our drinks and a basket of breadsticks. I can hear my trainer's voice screaming in the back of my mind about carbs and how I'm not going to the gym right now and all of that, but goddamn if those breadsticks don't smell like baked heaven.

I take one from the basket and tear it in half. It's too hot to eat. So much for using a full mouth as an excuse not to speak right away. Staring down at the steaming bread in my hands, I say, "I guess… I mean, L.A. is super expensive. Have you thought about going to another city to get started again?"

"Not really. Los Angeles has been home for so long, I can't imagine living anywhere else."

I expected that, but the lead ball of disappointment in my stomach happens anyway. "I guess I can understand that. I don't think I could live outside of Vegas."

"Really?"

I nod. "Been there my whole life. Bought a place and everything."

His eyebrows flick up. "You bought the place?"

"Yeah." I try not to let my defensiveness show. "Look, I know it's not the most glamorous place in the—"

"No, no." He waves his hand. As he reaches for a breadstick, he says, "I just hadn't realized you'd bought it. Seems like a smart investment, actually."

The defensiveness recedes a little bit. "It does?"

"Well yeah. Compared to renting, definitely. Your mortgage payment goes toward something you could sell later if you were so inclined." He shrugs. "So yeah, I think it's smart."

I swallow. "It's… I don't actually have a mortgage payment. I paid the place off a couple of years ago."

"No shit?"

"Yeah. I bought it when the market tanked, so I got it for like half what it's actually worth. Threw as much money as I could at it for like six or seven years, and now it's paid off."

"That's amazing. I should have done that with my condo." With a touch of bitterness, he adds, "My situation would be very, very different if I had. You're smart."

I shrug. "Not really. I just knew a lot of people who lost their shirts when the market crashed, so I was scared to be in debt. My rent kept going up, so I figured it made sense to buy something. At least this way, if I lose one of my jobs—or both of them—I still have a place to live, and I still have a car."

"Car's paid off too?"

"Yep."

He whistles, then laughs again. "You're definitely better at this than I am. I bought the condo, a brand new car, and then a brand new *sports* car on top of it. That's why everything fell apart after I lost my job. I couldn't afford to keep up on the mortgage. The bank repossessed the sports car, and after they foreclosed the condo, I had to sell the other car just so I could eat." His expression darkens. "That's…how I ended up in Vegas. I sold the car, and with the money I got from that, plus what I had left, I could either scrape by for a few more months or go blow it all and go out on a high." He picks up his glass. "I'd be in a lot better financial straits if I'd done things your way."

*And I wouldn't know you.*

I'm instantly mortified by my own thought. I'm glad we crossed paths, but if I had the power to go back and change things, I'd absolutely rather he'd stayed on level ground instead of coming to Vegas in the first place. Meeting him was a razor-thin silver lining around a violently destructive storm.

*But if that storm had to happen, I won't apologize for being thankful for that silver lining.*

I take a swallow of iced tea. "Live and learn, right?" It's stupid, but I don't know what else to say.

Max smiles. He holds my gaze and quietly says, "Yeah. Live and learn."

# Chapter 16
## Max

We both eat so much we damn near need to be rolled out of the restaurant. The food is spectacular, though, so I can't complain. Not even if it means neither of us will want to have sex tonight. Sometimes dinner is just worth it.

We don't go back to the room yet. Instead, Adrian lets me take the wheel and I show him around L.A. He's never been to Hollywood, so I take him out there. Sunset Strip. The Walk of Fame, though it's a little tough to see from the car. Grauman's Chinese Theatre. Some of the famous restaurants and some of the ones I used to frequent. The Hollywood Bowl, where I went to more concerts than I could count. The Hollywood sign, of course.

I even show him the complex where I used to live, and it doesn't hurt as much as I expect it to. It's been less than a year since the bank kicked me out, and it already feels like a place someone else used to live. Like we're looking up landmarks from a movie we've seen or I'm pointing out where some now-washed-up celebrity lived during their heyday rather than checking out the terrain of my old life. Which...there are plenty of celebrities in that building, and during my time there, I watched more than a few leave after their star faded and the money stopped flowing. Guess I should've taken that as a warning, but I'd always figured that kind of thing only happened to people in showbiz. Those of us with steady, normal jobs would be stable forever. Right. About that.

Despite the detachment from this place, Hollywood does start getting a little depressing, so I take him out to Santa Monica. It's half an hour or so past sunset, and we manage to find a place to park that isn't a hundred miles from the beach. From there, we walk a few blocks until pavement turns to sand.

The pier is, as usual, crowded. We head that way, but even after I've had time to digest some of that enormous dinner, the smell of funnel cakes and popcorn is enough to turn my stomach. Adrian looks a little green too, so we go toward the water instead.

There are still a few people hanging out on the sand, and that small crowd gets even thinner the farther we walk along the beach. In no time, we're completely alone, and aside from the lapping tide and the carnival music coming from the pier, it's quiet.

I take in a deep breath of the salty air. "*This* is one of the things I love about living here."

"I can see why. The lack of beaches is definitely not a selling point of Vegas."

I chuckle. "I'm surprised they haven't built one. There's got to be some casino tycoon out there who's designing a sandy saltwater beach, complete with a tide."

A laugh bursts out of Adrian, which makes my heart flutter. God, I love the way he smiles. Even in the dim light, his eyes sparkle.

Oblivious to me ogling him, he says, "You know, it wouldn't surprise me. With some of the shit they've built over the years..." He shakes his head. "Give it time."

"Seriously. That's a strange city you've got out there."

"Yeah, I know." His laughter fades a bit, but his smile doesn't. "It's home, though."

"Seems like you've got a pretty good thing going."

He eyes me like he thinks I'm being sarcastic. "Living in a double wide and stripping for money?"

"Your house is paid off. You seem to enjoy both of your jobs. You're at home there." I shrug. "Yeah, I'd say it's all good."

He relaxes again. I've noticed his hackles go up whenever we touch on his house or his job as a sex worker.

"You really do catch a lot of hell, don't you?" I ask. "For the way you live your life."

"You think?"

"I can tell."

He sighs, sliding his hands into his pockets and staring down at the sand as we keep walking. "It's weird. I'm not embarrassed by what I do or where I live. I'm not ashamed of any of it. In fact, I *like* my life. The house isn't much, but it's mine. The job isn't going to make me millions, but I'm good at it." He half shrugs. "Everyone just insists on having an *opinion* about it."

"I believe it. Everyone seems to have an opinion about everything other people are doing. And I can imagine it's a lot worse when there's sex involved."

"Yeah. But I knew what I was signing up for."

"Doesn't mean you have to like other people's bullshit."

He gives a little grunt of agreement but lets it drop.

We walk in comfortable silence for a while. In the back of my mind, I know this won't last forever. It won't even last much longer. His jobs are waiting in Vegas. Mine is... Well, hopefully I'll have one soon. Vegas is his home. L.A. is mine.

This? Temporary. Just like those nights I spent right over there on the pier, drinking and having fun with my friends during our high school and college days. Some nights felt like they'd never end. The summers always seemed like they'd last forever. Last time I went to the

151

pier—must've been three, four years ago now—the clunk of milk bottles being toppled by beanbags had stopped me in my tracks and taken me back to those younger days. I hadn't realized until that night just how much time had gone by since that era, and I'd caught myself trying to mentally track down all the people I used to hang out with. They were all scattered to the wind, though. The summers we'd never expected to end had not only ended, they'd faded to barely visible black and white. Like one of those old photos that's so degraded you can't even read the description someone wrote on the back.

I realize now that eventually, there will come a time when something will remind me of this time with Adrian. Maybe someone with vivid blue eyes or a particularly talented stripper or a homeless guy on the street. Something will trip the synapses in my brain where this period is stored. I wonder how I'll react when that happens. When enough time has gone by that Adrian is a distant memory and something brings him back to the front of my mind.

My throat tightens a little at the thought of Adrian being so far away that I have to stop and think to bring his name to the tip of my tongue.

Without really thinking about it—and perhaps against my better judgment—I take his hand. His slim fingers are cool, and they separate easily to let mine curl over the back of his hand. After another couple of steps, his fingers curl too, resting the pads against my skin.

We glance at each other. We both smile. The tide keeps lapping at the sand. The carnival sounds of Santa Monica Pier keep slowly fading behind us. And for tonight, here in Los Angeles, Adrian isn't a faded photograph tucked into a box of mementos. He's real. I memorize every detail of him and about now, from the way his hair keeps fluttering into his eyes to the grain of sand that's slipped down into my shoe.

Adrian's gait slows. After a few more steps, he halts. I do too, and for a moment, we face each other in silence. He's difficult to see, especially with his back to the lights of the city, but he's just visible enough to be distinctly Adrian. Sharp cheekbones. Smooth jaw line. Dark hair fluttering in the breeze.

He frees his hand from mine and, to my surprise, wraps his arms around my neck. Mine move of their own volition and snake around his waist, and he takes a step closer so we're pressed against each other. Then he kisses me, and no, this is not a night that will ever fade into nothing. This will be one of those nights I remember when I'm a hundred.

I hold him tight and let him guide everything. His kiss is languid, like he isn't even thinking this could turn into more. It's impossible not to be aroused when I'm kissing him, but at the same time, this is the least sexual kiss we've ever shared. It's just tender and affectionate, his lips and tongue moving lazily with mine, and it's perfect.

It feels like hours before we finally come up for air. The city seems darker now, and quieter. The pier is so far away I can barely hear the music and noise. Even the tide seems to have backed away, like the ocean itself wants to give us some privacy.

"For what it's worth," I whisper against his lips, "I could do without how my life has gone over the last year." I tame a few strands of his hair and stroke them down into place. "But it's a little easier to swallow when I realize it's the reason I met you."

Adrian just smiles.

"Is it weird that I wish this could go on a little longer?"

"No." He kisses me again, just his lips this time. "I know you need to start working and getting your life together. But...I have really enjoyed, you know, this." He draws back enough that if it were light out, I'd be able to see his eyes. "It's been a long time since I've been with someone who knows what I am and treats me like a human. So…thank you for that."

My breath hitches. It's so bizarre to imagine that the man who picked me up off the sidewalk—after literally *thousands* of people walked past me—is so surprised when someone treats *him* like a human being.

I cup his cheek, loving the warmth of his skin and the slight abrasiveness of his five o'clock shadow against my palm. "You're going to have to come up with something a lot worse than being a sex worker to change the way I look at you."

"I don't think I want to try to come up with something like that." He lifts his chin and lets our lips brush. "I like the way you look at me."

"Yeah. Me too."

And then I kiss him again before I say too much.

# Chapter 17
## Adrian

Thanks to a series of long, indulgent kisses, it's late by the time we get back to the car. Thanks to some late night traffic, it's a good hour and a half beyond that before we're back at the motel.

We're both a little drowsy by the time Max pulls my car into the parking lot, but the click of the key card in the reader at our room gives us both a second wind. As soon as we're inside, Max pushes me up against the door and kisses me, and it's not the way we were kissing on the beach. He's practically shaking now, running his hands all over me and kissing me deeply.

I'm a mess myself, and the thick ridge of his cock getting harder against mine is going to make me lose my damned mind. Now that there's no one around to see us, there's no reason to hold back.

"Get... Clothes..." I can't speak, and it's not just because I'm trying to kiss him at the same time. Even when I force myself to break the kiss, all I can articulate is, "Naked."

Max groans in response and rubs his now fully hard erection against me. "Yeah. Good idea." Then he kisses me again. We're no closer to separating now, but at least our hands seem to be on the right track. Mine are trying to remember how the buttons of his shirt operate. His are somehow getting my belt undone.

Piece by piece, we drop clothes on the floor or toss them over the tops of boxes. We leave a trail of shoes from the door to the bed. He still has on underwear as we pull back the covers and get into bed, but that doesn't last long either, and finally, I have Max exactly how I want him—naked, horizontal, and against me.

The way we kiss now is the most amazing combination of that first time in the strip club and tonight on the beach. It's hot and needy, exactly what I'd expect from two men on a collision course with a couple of powerful orgasms. Somehow, though, it's also sweet and gentle. Like we're both turned on within an inch of our lives but still absolutely aware that we aren't just two guys trying to get each other off. I can't forget—and I don't want to—that this is *Max*. The way he holds me and touches me, I get the feeling he's completely aware this is me.

Max rolls me onto my back, and my shoulder blades have barely hit the sheets before he's kissing his way down my neck and onto my chest. He's not doing that straight shot downward to suck me off, either—he's definitely taking the scenic route. I can't remember the last time someone paid so much attention to my nipple, or the last time I was so fucking turned on by what a guy did to it. With just his lips, teeth, and tongue, he's got my nipple so hard it could cut diamonds, and I'm arching and gasping with every touch and sweep and gentle bite. Then he moves to the other one and starts all over again.

"Oh my God, Max," I breathe, raking my fingers through his hair. "Fuck that's so good."

He growls quietly, and keeps at it. Squeezing my eyes shut, I squirm under him, and every time I lift my hips, my dick brushes his stomach, and we both moan.

He gives my nipple one last lick, then continues down, and he's still not in any hurry. It's like he's fascinated with how my muscles move every time he kisses or licks my abs, and I'm so lightheaded and turned on, I couldn't stop them from quivering or contracting if I wanted to. Which I don't. Because holy fuck, I love how he makes me feel.

His lips skate over my tattoo, and it's a tad ticklish when they follow the underside of the dragon. Lifting his head, he says, "You've got a scar there?" Not disgust. Just curiosity.

"Y-yeah." I sweep my tongue across my lips. "Appendix scar."

"Nice cover-up."

I laugh, and I wonder if I sound as drunk as I feel. "Clients don't…like scars."

"Idiots," he mutters, more to himself. He flicks his tongue along the middle of the scar, where the thick ridge stands out the most. "The tattoo is sexy as hell, though."

"Thanks." I'm pretty sure it comes out clearly, but his arm grazes my very hard and very neglected cock, and my brain melts.

And he picks just that moment—right when I'm about to fall to pieces anyway—to shift position and give my dick a long, slow lick from base to tip.

"Oh *God*," I moan. "That's so—fuck!"

He's deep-throating me now. Zero to sixty in no time flat. His lips squeeze and his tongue flutters and circles and does things it shouldn't even be physically able to do, and I don't even know how I'm still on the bed instead of levitating up to the damn ceiling. I've got both hands in his hair, kneading and pulling and combing, and it's like everything is focused between my legs—Max's mouth on my cock, my hands in his hair, all this intense and overwhelming sensation. It's so hot and almost perfect. Jesus. The only thing missing is—

"Want to kiss you." The words tumble out. I don't take them back. No matter how much I love his mouth on my cock, now that I've said it, I do want to kiss him. A lot. I want to make out and rub against him and feel him all over until he's covered in cum, and at the rate he's going, that last part's not going to take long. *"Please."*

He stops so suddenly I gasp, and a second later, he's over me. Now we're kissing *violently*. Teeth clack together now and then, and who the fuck cares? He's pulling the breath right out of me, and I rake my nails up his back, and he rewards me with the most delicious groan and a full-body shudder, which rubs his dick against mine. God, yeah, I love this. I scratch him again, and he once against shudders against me. I rock my hips a little, and he takes the hint and starts thrusting against me.

Abruptly, though, he stops. "Too much friction." He looks around. "Where's the lube?"

"Table." I motion toward his side of the bed. He lunges for it, and when he comes back, he fumbles with the bottle. I try to help, but my hands aren't any steadier, and suddenly we go from a stubbornly closed bottle to lube *everywhere*. It spurts past his hand and onto my chest like an epic money shot, and we both stop.

He looks down at the strip of lube. Our eyes meet. And we both burst out laughing.

"Well." I run my hand along the spilled liquid to scoop up as much as I can. "Guess we're taking a shower after this."

"Guess we—hey!" He laughs as I smear the lube down his chest. "Wrong place."

"Oh." I bat my eyes. "Oops?"

We both chuckle, and pour some more lube into our hands. Now it's going where it belongs—on our cocks. We stroke it onto each other, and he's rocking his hips again, sliding against our hands and my cock. I smear some more of the excess on his stomach, and he chuckles and leaves a nice long trail of it down my thigh. I laugh, and so does he, and somehow we're laughing between kissing, thrusting together in between smearing lube everywhere, and it's hot and playful and sexy and messy, and holy fuck, I'm so dizzy I really do feel like I'm drunk.

"Oh God," he moans, and I recognize that voice. He's getting close. His thrusts are erratic and frantic now, slippery skin sliding over mine, and when he starts cursing, the throaty helplessness drives me wild. I hold onto his shoulders as I can with lubed up hands and push my hips up against his, staying with him even though his rhythm is all over the place. Fuck, I'm getting there too—my orgasm's closing in, and I whimper as I thrust for all I'm worth.

"Oh shit... oh... *yeah!*" It's me this time, the words falling out of my mouth even though I don't even remember breathing. "Don't stop. God, Max, don't stop."

He makes a sound that's probably supposed to be words—hell if I can understand it—but he absolutely doesn't stop, and the bed is shaking so hard I'm surprised the whole room isn't shaking. Or maybe it is. There could be a freight train going by and an earthquake happening, and the only thing I'm aware of is this gorgeous man fucking against me, slippery skin sliding against slippery skin, and—

Max shudders hard, and I'm coming even before the first drop of his cum lands on my skin. Rhythm and thrusting are a distant memory, and we just tremble and jerk until neither of us has anything left.

He collapses on top of me. I pull him down until our chests—lube, cum, sweat, and all—are pressed together, though he does hold himself up enough to let me breathe.

Everything is silent now. The earthquake is over. The freight train is gone. The bed isn't going to fall to pieces. It's all still, quiet, and calm.

Max kisses my cheek. "Definitely going to need a shower."

I laugh. "Yeah. You're right."

"In a minute." He lets head fall beside mine, and buries his face against my neck. "Don't think I can move yet."

"No rush." I close my eyes and stroke his hair. Of course there's lube on my hand, but… Hell, we're taking a shower soon. So…whatever.

For the moment, I just want to lie here and hold him.

*Might as well enjoy it while I can.*

The thought tries to shake me out of my post-coital bliss and depress the hell out of me, but I shove it away. I can think about that later.

Right now, nothing exists except this.

~*~

That whole "think about it later" thing?

It doesn't wait very long.

Max is out cold beside me. Once we'd finished our shower, our evening caught up with us. The big meal. The wild sex. The late hour. We both had just enough energy left to dry off, stagger back to bed, and collapse.

I slept for a little while, but now it's two-thirty, and I'm wide awake and thinking about last night with a ball of lead in my gut.

Between dinner and the walk on the beach and the sex, I almost fooled myself into believing this thing we're doing is something. I mean, it's not *nothing*, but I'm an idiot if I think it's love.

*Love? Who said anything about love?*

I close my eyes and wipe my hand over my face. Okay, so maybe my brain hadn't gotten that far yet, but I can't imagine it would've taken long for that word to start bouncing around in my skull. And why not? Max is the sweetest guy I've met in a long time. The connection with him is… It's like I don't remember him ever being a stranger.

But he also thanks me for helping him and tries to pay me back at every opportunity. It's not that I think he's having sex with me out of obligation, or that he's not being genuinely nice to me, but where is the line where it stops being gratitude and starts being a *real* connection? I don't know. I've tried like hell, and I can't find that line.

I turn on my side and watch him sleep. There's enough light coming in from the parking lot to illuminate his silhouette, and his chest rises and falls slowly with long, deep breaths. I'm glad he's getting sleep. In his shoes, I'd be too stressed to sleep, and I'd spend all night sweating over my situation.

Sort of like I'm doing right now over our relationship.

Relationship? That's a bit of a stretch. He needs help, I'm giving him help, and we happen to have some pretty awesome sex in between. I'm kidding myself if I think he's in any state of mind to fall in love with anyone, never mind someone like me.

I sigh, fighting the urge to touch him just for the hell of it. No sense waking him up, though as deep as he seems to be sleeping, a marching band couldn't disturb him. Still, I won't take any chances.

And anyway, I'd just be making it harder for myself. The fact is, every time I touch him, I want to touch him more. Every night we spend together makes it that much harder for me to face the reality that I'm going back to Las Vegas soon. Just like when I dropped him off at the bus station and then found myself facing the prospect of dropping him off again. If a second goodbye under the Greyhound sign would've been hard, this is going to be hell.

Which means, I realize with a sinking feeling, that the sooner I walk away, the less it'll hurt when I do. It's still going to hurt like hell no matter what, but maybe not *as* bad.

Tomorrow. I need to leave tomorrow. Or, well, today. And the earlier the better so I can avoid some of L.A.'s brutal traffic.

I lift myself up enough to glance at the alarm clock on his side of the bed. It's almost three.

If I leave now, I'll miss the worst of it.

If I leave now, I might even miss some of the worst traffic in Vegas.

If I leave now, I might be able to talk myself into going through with it.

Without another thought, I swing my legs over the side of the bed, reach for my overnight bag, and start getting ready to go.

# Chapter 18
## Max

The room isn't pitch black, but it's definitely still dark out. The only light coming in is from the streetlights.

There's movement in the room, though.

Rubbing my eyes, I start to sit up. Then I blink a few times and look around until I find the source.

Adrian has his back to me. He's dressed, and he's putting some things into a box. No, that's not right—his overnight bag is sitting on top of the box, and his toiletry kit is next to it.

My heart jumps into my throat. "What are you doing?"

He startles and freezes. Then, without looking at me, he continues what he's doing. "I need to go." His tone is flat but not completely steady, and my blood turns cold.

I turn on the bedside lamp, flinching away from the sudden brightness. As my eyes adjust, I watch him. "You need to go? Why?"

He stops again, and his shoulders sink. "Max, we…"

More ice slithers through my veins. I get up, grab my boxers off the floor, and pull them on. "Adrian, talk to me."

He finally turns around. The circles under his eyes are a little heavier, and he just looks exhausted. "I need to. We're... Things are getting too intense."

*So it wasn't just me.*

I swallow and come closer, but he stiffens, so I stop. "What do you mean?"

"I mean..." He drops his gaze. After a moment, he sighs and sits on the foot of the bed, shoulders sagging a bit more as fatigue radiates off him. "This thing we're doing—it's temporary, you know?" He meets my eyes again, and I swear his are begging me to understand. "You'll get your life going again, and I'll go back to mine, and..." He throws up his hands. "That's it."

"It doesn't have to be."

Adrian exhales. "Yeah, it does. We just met. You're still finding your footing. And besides, this city is home to you. Vegas"—he motions in the general direction of the city—"is to me. We could do the long distance thing for a while, and then what? Break up when it gets to be too much effort?"

"Too much effort?" I blink. "Seems like it would be *worth* the effort."

Adrian laughs bitterly. He gets up and starts putting the last couple of things—neatly folded T-shirts—into his bag. "That's easy to say now," he says over his shoulder. "When the novelty of dating a guy like me wears off, you'll probably change your tune."

"What do you mean, a guy like you?" I finally close the last little bit of distance between us and reach for his arm. For the first time since I've known him, he recoils.

"Max." He blows out a breath and stuffs his toiletry kit into the bag. "You're a great guy. I could absolutely see myself getting attached to you. I...kind of already am." He zips the bag before he turns to me. "But that doesn't mean we can make this work. It's easy for you to say now that you don't mind me being a sex worker, but give it some time. Think about all the colleagues you're reconnecting with or the ones you'll meet at your job." Adrian shakes his head. "You really want them to know you're dating a stripper?"

I stare at him in disbelief. "Adrian, I—"

"Don't." He puts up a hand and shakes his head again. "I wanted to help you get home, and I did. Now *I* need to get home." He swallows with what seems like some work and pulls the bag onto his shoulder. "I need to go before traffic gets bad."

I start to speak again, but his expression cuts me off. He's not angry, not hostile. In fact, that would be easier to handle. If anything, his eyes are filled with bone-deep hurt, and everything in his face and his body language says that if I keep talking, I'm just going to make that hurt cut deeper. I don't want to let him go, but I can't do that either.

I clear my throat. "Okay. If… If that's what you need to do."

He nods. He looks toward the door, and a lump rises in my throat because I know this is so close to over and I'm not ready for it.

"Thank you again," I whisper. "For everything."

He meets my gaze, and the faintest hint of a smile pulls at his lips. "You're welcome." We hold eye contact for one, two, three seconds, and as soon as he breaks it, I can almost literally feel him slipping through my fingers. He adjusts the strap on his shoulder, starts for the door, and…

And he's gone.

Out the door. Keys jingling. Car door slamming. Gone.

My chest aches as I sink back onto the bed. It was stupid for me to get so attached to him. We've only known each other a matter of days. And it's not like I fell in love with him.

I just know that if he'd stayed a *little* bit longer, I would have.

~*~

It takes another week and a couple more job interviews for an offer to come through. It's not the cushy-ass six-figure gig I had before, but it means I can get things like food and a place to live. Right now, I'm staying in my old colleague's spare bedroom, and hopefully I'll be out of his hair before too much longer.

The new job isn't bad. I know most of the senior people in the department from the industry, and everything seems to run like the proverbial well-oiled machine. They've got a new ad campaign coming through for a special edition brand of sneakers from one of the bigger companies. Apparel was never really my area of expertise, but I'm not too worried about it.

A month goes by. I'm settling in. I even have a piece of shit car that has the cheapest and most basic insurance available. Next step—an apartment. That might be a couple of months down the line, but it's feeling more possible than it has in ages.

I'm back in Los Angeles and back in my career field, and I swear that any day now, I might feel like I'm back in my own skin.

Except I don't.

Sometimes I drive into Hollywood to see if I feel some sort of something from my old stomping grounds. Regret? Sadness? Nostalgia?

Nothing. It's like driving through a neighborhood I've seen in postcards. All the signs and buildings are more or less the same, but they mean nothing to me. There's no connection beyond vague recognition. I don't feel a thing.

Not until I go out to Santa Monica one night and take a walk down the beach.

It's no surprise when I'm flooded with memories and emotions with Adrian's name all over them. It's like the sky's just opened up and started dumping rain on me, and there's nothing I can do but stand here and let it. Or rather, there's nothing I want to do. This hurts like hell, but it's better than the numb autopilot I've been running on.

I sit on the sand and stare out at the lights glinting on the dark water. A couple walk by, and I self-consciously turn away and make the subtlest gesture possible of wiping my eyes. I doubt they can even see me, and they probably couldn't give two shits. I should be used to that, too. God knows enough people walked on by me on the streets in Vegas.

Thousands of people.

And one stopped.

And now he's gone.

And without him, everything is just...blank.

It's stupid for him to have that much of a hold on me. That him leaving has sucked all the color out of my life and turned me into a mindless drone who just goes to work, does his job, comes home, and does it all over again.

A thought drops into my head, and I freeze.

It's not that Adrian came along and took all the color out. It's not that I turned into a drone after he left.

There *was* no color before him. I *was* a drone. Not because I was waiting for him to come along so my life was worth living, but because I'd been living for my job and nothing else. I was that drone for a long, long time before Adrian came into the picture. He was a taste of something that had never been here before. Something beautiful that's missing now.

I stand up and turn around so I can see the city. This skyline is as familiar as my own reflection. It's been home for as long as I can remember.

So why doesn't it feel like that anymore?

I close my eyes and take in a long breath through my nose. I still love the smell of the sea, but it's not that soft cologne Adrian sometimes wears. I love the noise and the bustle of the city, but it's not lying in bed and seeing someone there who makes my pulse go crazy. I love the city's vibe, but it's not Adrian's playful—if sometimes self-conscious—personality or that addictive laugh.

I love Los Angeles.

But this isn't my home anymore.

I open my eyes, give the city one last look, and head back up the beach toward the car. I need to go get some sleep.

Because tomorrow, I'm going to make some phone calls.

# Chapter 19
## Adrian

I never thought I'd hate stripping, but I do.

In the beginning, it was fun when guys leered and threw money. They may have thought I was there for their entertainment—which I was—but I always had the power. The upper hand. When I strip, I give or withhold what they want. If they have enough money, I might even give them a little more. In their eyes, I'm a piece of meat, but at the end of the day, they're the dogs drooling and hoping they *might* get a nibble. It's always been a hell of a rush for me, letting them fall all over themselves and beg while I decide who gets what.

Ever since I came back from L.A., it hasn't been the same. It's hard to get a thrill from a leer now that I know what it's like to dance for someone who looks at me like Max did. He was hard and definitely turned on when I gave him that lap dance, but he still gazed up at me almost *reverently*. It's like I went from eating crappy diner steaks to a three hundred dollar Michelin-starred filet mignon, and now I've lost my taste for the cheap shit.

These days, when I take guys back into the private booths, I can't help thinking that if I gave any one of them the green light for some touching, it won't be a caress to my face.

I need to get over it. It's been almost two months since I came back to Las Vegas. There's no reason I should still be dreading my shifts at the NightOwl.

At least I'm not working there tonight. I'm at the tables, and I can still work up the enthusiasm to deal cards. The first week or two was a bit rough because I kept catching myself looking for Max in the crowd, but once I'd get into a groove, I was good.

Tonight it's pretty quiet. Right now my table is empty. For most of the evening, I've had at most three people. One guy in particular was in the same chair when I relieved the other dealer two hours ago, and he only left in the last couple of minutes. Poor guy just kept throwing ten-dollar chips on each hand, hitting when he should've stayed, doubling down when he should've hit, staying when he should've split. Dude did not know how to play blackjack, and every time anyone offered him advice, he'd brush it off and tell us he knew what he was doing. I can't help wondering if he's trying to blow his cash so he can finish himself off like Max.

Max. God. My mind just keeps going back to him. Everything reminds me of him. I can't even walk by the Bellagio anymore and started going a different way back to my car from the NightOwl. The coffee mug he used, the couch he slept on, the logo on a pizza box from Antonio's—I can't get away from him.

This is stupid. We've been apart longer than we were together. Leaving was hard, but it was the right thing to do, and sooner or later, my idiot brain will catch up.

On the bright side, meeting him shook me out of that apathy I'd developed toward the homeless on the Strip. A week after I got back, I started volunteering at the homeless shelter twice a week. It isn't much, but I hope it helps them as much as it soothes my conscience.

I absently play with a couple of five hundred-dollar chips just to give my restless hands something to do. I could really stand for the casino to get a hell of a lot busier so I don't have quite so much downtime right now. The tips would be nice too. But mostly, I'd like to have something to do besides—

Someone slides into the chair directly across from me, and I instantly put on my game face and—

Blink.

Stupidly.

"Max?" I manage after a couple of mute seconds. "What are you doing here?"

He smiles shyly, brow pinched like it is whenever he's nervous. "I was hoping to talk to you for a few minutes. Either here, or if you've got a break coming up." He swallows. "If...you *want* to talk, I mean."

I'm so shocked that he's even here, I haven't decided yet if I want to take him up on it, or if it's a good idea. "What... What about?"

He holds my gaze. "I think you know."

My heart speeds up. The unspoken "*us*" is so loud, I'm surprised the scattered crowd of gamblers doesn't collectively turn and stare. "We... Max, there's no point. We're—"

"Just hear me out. Please. After that, if you want me to go, I will." He shows his palms. "Promise."

Fuck. *Fuck.* This is not going to help me get over him.

But the sooner we get it over with, the sooner I can get back to trying. So, I turn and wave for Kelly, the pit boss. She switches me out with Kenny, a dealer who's still learning the job, and she hovers over him while I step out with Max.

Privacy is hard to come by in a casino, and I can't take him into the restricted areas for employees, so I settle for the parking garage. We're still in plain view of several eyes in the sky, but at least we're not on the crowded casino floor.

"Okay." I fold my arms across my chest and face him. "So, what's this about?"

He takes a deep breath. "I had a job interview today." His Adam's apple bobs. "In Henderson."

I blink. "As in, just-down-the-road Henderson?"

Max nods. "They made me an offer." He sets his jaw and holds my gaze. "And it's up to you if I accept it or not."

"I…" I shake myself. "I'm not following. What's going on?"

He studies me. Then he exhales, and it's like he's exhausted just from holding himself upright. He stays on his feet, but sways a little like he just wants to collapse. "I'm miserable in L.A. It's…" He shakes his head. "It's not home anymore. I'm not sure if it ever really was. Or if I've ever known what that even means. For sixteen years, I lived and breathed my career to the point that I stopped living at all. Being with you was…" He swallows again and looks me in the eye. "That was the closest to alive I've ever felt."

I'm completely speechless, my heart thumping and my stomach flipping over and over.

He goes on. "I thought at first it was because I'd come so close to suicide. Anything that wasn't dying or being on the street is pretty good. Except…it was more than that. Looking back, I realized I've been living in black and white, and suddenly you showed up in Technicolor." He's struggling to hold my gaze, and his voice wavers as he says, "I want the color back."

All the air gets lost on its way to my lungs.

Max moistens his lips. "If you aren't interested, say the word, and I'm on my way back to Los Angeles." He steps a little closer, which makes it even harder to breathe. "But if you want to give this thing a shot, I'm here."

I cough into my fist. "Is… Is it even a job you want?"

"It's a paycheck." He shrugs. "There's only two things I want right now—stability, and you. If it turns out it's not a job I want to do forever, I can get another one. But there's only one you."

I'm mute again for almost a minute and finally sputter, "You came all this way and found a job...just so you can be with me?"

Max nods.

I want to ask him why. I want to ask him what the hell he's thinking. I want to grab him by the shoulders, shake him, and ask him how in the world this seemed like a good idea.

But he's looking at me like that again.

The way he did at the club. On the beach. Right before I left. He's looking at me like nothing else exists in his entire world.

Like there's nothing else he wants.

I clear my throat again, this time to get rid of the sudden ache. "You're crazy."

He laughs quietly, and shrugs. "So I've been told." Sobering, he inches a little closer, and his voice is low and serious when he speaks again. "I was crazy for letting so many years of my life go by. And with as much as I've been hurting since you left, I know I'd be crazy not to at least try this. I don't know if we can make it work. I just know I have too many regrets already, and I don't want to add letting you go to that list." He pauses. "If it's a no, then say the word, and I'll leave. That's why I haven't accepted the job offer. I only want this if you do too."

Tears prick at my eyes. "You... You're serious about all this. I've never even been worth someone's effort as a boyfriend, but you...really came back...for *me*?"

"You're absolutely worth the effort. I couldn't forget about you and move on, and it's because I don't want to. I want to put in the effort and see what this can turn into." In a shaky whisper so soft I barely hear it, he adds, "I've missed you, Adrian. More than you can imagine."

"No, I..." I step closer and slide a hand around the back of his neck. "I'm pretty sure I can."

And just like that, I'm back where I've been dying to be for the last few weeks—wrapped up in Max's arms with his lips pressed to mine. I don't remember him ever holding me quite this tight, but I'm not about to complain.

*Don't you dare let me go this time.*

The kiss lasts for God knows how long, but much too soon, he breaks it and touches his forehead to mine. "So, does this mean I should take the job?"

I laugh, and a few tears slip free. "Yeah. It does."

He smiles against my lips, then kisses me again.

When we finally loosen our embrace, our eyes meet. His are as wet as mine, so I don't feel quite as ridiculous now.

"I, um…" I clear my throat and glance back toward the elevators. "I can probably get my boss to let me out early. It's pretty dead tonight."

"It's up to you." He smiles and caresses my face, sending a shiver all the way down to my curling toes. "I'm staying a couple of blocks off the Strip, but it's not too far. I can meet you later if—"

"No." I shake my head. "As much as I've been dying to see you again, I'd rather not wait."

Max smiles again. "Your call."

I kiss him once more, then gesture toward the elevators. "Let me go up and weasel out of my shift. Then maybe we can go back to my place."

The smile turns to a grin. "I like that idea."

"I'll be right back."

# Chapter 20
## Max

*This is what it feels like to come home.*

That's all I can think as Adrian and I sink onto his bed, naked and tangled up in each other. It's a wonder I haven't broken down in tears—I've been so emotionally on-edge for weeks now, even after I got the ball rolling to find a job over here, and today I was almost sick with nerves before I approached him. I'd convinced myself more than once that I was wasting my time, that he was done with me, and that there was no way in hell this night would end in his bed.

And yet, here we are.

I'm on my back, which means my hands are free to roam his beautiful body as we kiss like it's been years—not weeks—since the last time we touched. My God, I can't believe we're here, and he's on top of me, and he's breathing hard the way he does when he's this turned on.

"Tell me what you want," I whisper between kisses. "Anything."

"Hmm." His lips curve into a grin against mine. "I do want to fuck you one of these days."

I moan at the thought of his cock inside me. "One of these days, like now?"

175

It's his turn to moan, and he shivers, pressing that thick erection against my hip. "You don't mind switching?"

"Mind? Oh God no." I grasp his hips and pull him harder against me. "I kept meaning to suggest it before, but I was having so much fun topping you."

Adrian laughs. Holy fuck, but that's the sweetest thing I've heard in too long. I love his smile, his laugh…

"Fuck me," I whisper. "Right now."

"Mmm, I love it when you get bossy," he purrs.

I laugh and squeeze his perfect ass. "You're going to love it even more when I turn over and let you fuck me."

"Let me?" He snorts. "Weren't you just ordering me to? Which is it?"

"Why don't you get a condom and find out?"

"Well when you put it like that…" He climbs off me and gets a condom and lube from the bedside table. As if I wasn't crazy aroused before—the prospect of taking him makes my mouth water. Jesus fuck.

He rolls on the condom, then looks at me. "How long as it been since you've done this?"

"A while." I move closer to him and tease his balls with my fingertips. "Just go slow to start with, and I'll be fine."

He sucks in a breath, closing his eyes as I play with him. "I can go slow. Definitely."

"To *start* with, I said." I lean in and nibble on his nipple, which makes him yelp and shiver. "You tease me too much, you'll pay for it."

"Oh yeah?"

"Mmhmm."

"Hmm. I might have to take my chances." He lifts my chin and kisses me. "For right now, though, either you turn around, or I take off this condom and fuck your mouth."

"Oh, that's tempting too, so—"

"Turn around. *Now.*"

I don't argue. As I turn onto my hands and knees, Adrian climbs up behind me. The click of the lube bottle sends a zing of excitement right up my spine. It *has* been a while since I've bottomed. Too long. Not so long that I'm worried it'll hurt or something. I just can't wait another second.

Eyes closed, I let my head fall forward and try to be patient. I want him. I want him so bad. So, *so* bad. "C'mon…"

Adrian gives a wicked laugh. Damn it. Begging was a bad idea. He's going to make me work for it, isn't he?

A slick fingertip teases my hole. Circles, but no pressure. Son of a…

"Adrian. For God's sake."

"Something wrong?" His devilish grin is audible. Hot and frustrating at the same time. "You're not getting impatient, are you?"

I lean back against his finger, but of course, it doesn't help. And he laughs again. Fucking bastard.

I'm about to growl another demand-slash-plea for him to put *something* in me when his fingertip presses in. First firmly, then harder, and my vision blurs as not one but two fingers slide inside. "Oh yeah…"

"Like that?" That grin. That damn grin. He knows I like it.

"Want more." I lean back to drive his fingers deeper, and this time he lets me, and he bends them just right to hit that sweet spot. Dear God. At this rate, I won't last long enough for him to fuck me.

My cock desperately needs attention, so even though I know it'll speed things along, I start stroking just to take the edge off.

"You're getting ahead of me," he says, sliding his fingers in and out. "Don't come before the main event."

I bite my lip. "Gotta do something."

"Mmm." His other hand drifts up my side. "So what you're saying is, you're really turned on and want to be fucked."

The sound I make isn't English—probably barely even human—but I'm pretty sure it communicates the *yes*.

"Good thing I want to fuck you too." There's finally a note of desperation in his voice too, and we both moan as he withdraws his fingers. I have just enough time to take a breath, and he's pressing his cock against me. "This good? Not hurting you?"

"No. Doesn't hurt." I dig the heel of my free hand into the mattress and lean back again.

"Oh God," he breathes as the head of his cock breaches me. "Fuck, I knew this would be…" He trails off into a moan.

"More." I squeeze my own cock, resisting the urge to stroke. "Please, more."

Adrian moans, and he's not teasing anymore. He works himself deeper, and I rock my hips to encourage more, and before I know it, we're moving in the most perfect unison, his cock slamming into me as I stroke myself and beg him for more, more, more.

"You feel so good," he breathes. "Oh God…"

"So… So do you." And through the haze of arousal, I realize just how amazing this is because not only does my body feel spectacular, but I'm with Adrian. I'm in his bed. I'm taking his cock. I'm here, and this is real.

The reality of it nearly drives me to simultaneous tears and an orgasm. There's sex, there's sex with Adrian, and there's sex with Adrian after I was convinced it would never happen again.

I need to see him. To make absolutely sure this is really him and he's really here. "W-wait."

He slows down. "What? You okay?"

I nod. "I'm good. Just…" Christ, I can't talk.

He leans forward and wraps his arm around my stomach. "Talk to me."

"I want…" I turn my head, and suddenly we're almost face to face. Close enough. I let go of my cock and reach up to grab the back of his neck. He doesn't resist at all, and the second our lips met, he thrusts deeper. There isn't much range of motion from this angle, but he uses every bit of it, and we're kissing, and fucking, and I don't know how I'm even still conscious. Much more of this and…

And…

"Oh God!" I 'break the kiss and let my head fall forward again, and Adrian doesn't miss a beat. He kisses my neck and pounds me—fucking *pounds* me—as much as he can like this, and he's hitting every nerve ending just right to drive me wild, and everything is turning blurry, so I just close my eyes anyway and enjoy the ride. I'm not even touching myself anymore, but it doesn't matter. I'm so close, right on the edge, ready to come, and—

He kisses the side of my neck, and releases a low, helpless moan, and I lose it.

"Fuck!" I buck under him, and he keeps riding me hard while I come, and then he's groaning in my ear as his cock pulses inside me.

I collapse onto my stomach. He comes down with me. He pauses to pull out but then sinks over me and kisses my shoulder.

"That was amazing," he slurs.

"Tell me 'bout it."

He presses his lips just beneath my hairline. "I'm really glad you came back."

I close my eyes and exhale. "Me too." And I swear to God, that's even more of a relief than the orgasm I just had. Relieving the sexual tension was hot, but this? Coming back to the same place? It's like I can *breathe* again.

We separate, and he takes care of the condom while I flop uselessly onto my back. A moment later, he's beside me, cuddling up against my chest where he still fits just as perfectly as he did before. Everything's exactly like it was the first time we found ourselves here in the middle of his bed after we'd fucked. It's like we never left.

I'm not sure how much time goes by. Several minutes at least. Maybe more. All I know is it's a long time between when we settle like this and Adrian breaks the silence.

"I missed you, by the way."

I press a kiss to his temple. "I missed you too."

He shifts around and lifts himself onto his elbow. Draping his other arm across my chest, he says, "You're really going to take the job in Henderson?"

"I think so." I tuck his hair behind his ear. I can't believe how much I missed doing that. "If it's not too weird for me to move to your city."

"Not for me, no. It's not like you're moving in with me." He pauses, smiling cautiously. "Yet."

I smile back and lift my head to kiss him. "One thing at a time."

Adrian nods. "What would you have done if I'd said no?"

"I still have a gig in L.A."

"So you didn't have a whole lot to lose?" He smirks, and the comment is playful, but there's a hint of uneasiness too.

"Careerwise? No." I run the backs of my fingers along his jaw. "Personally? Yeah. I'd say there was a hell of a lot to lose."

He holds my gaze, then comes in for a long, sweet kiss. Funny how I'd known all the way here from L.A. just how much was on the line, but now that I actually have him in my arms, it's like I didn't know the half of it. We weren't even supposed to cross paths and wouldn't have if I hadn't had my meltdown a few months ago. The fact that we made it back here…

I hold him tighter.

He breaks the kiss and looks in my eyes. "I'm sorry about leaving, too. It… At the time, I…"

"Adrian." I run my thumb along his lower lip. "I get it. I do. And I think it was for the better in the end. I needed the wakeup call, you know? To really think about what was going on. What it was, and…what it wasn't."

He studies me, searching my eyes for a moment. "So, what do you think it is?"

"Only one way to find out." I pause. "Seriously, I don't know. I just know I want to see where it could go. I'd rather give it a shot and have it not work out than spend the rest of my life wondering what might have been."

Something in Adrian seems to relax. Something that I think has been tense since the very beginning.

"Same here." He slides closer to me. "And it's been killing me ever since I left. I don't even know how many times I damn near turned around and came back that day."

"I think we both needed some time to figure it out, though. It was rough, but everything worked out."

He smiles again, a hint of shyness in his expression. "It did." Then that smile starts to fade, but the shyness doesn't. There's something else in his expression now. Something I can't quite put my finger on.

"What's wrong?"

He chews his lip for a moment. "You're changing jobs so we can be together. But…what does all this mean for *my* job?"

"For your—" The piece drops into place. "You think I want you to quit stripping."

"Most people don't want to date someone who—"

"Adrian. I'm not putting any conditions on this. You were stripping when I met you, and it's never occurred to me to ask you to stop."

"But can you really look me in the eye and tell me it doesn't bother you that I'm taking off my clothes and dancing in other men's laps?"

I give it some thought, and shrug. "No. I mean, I…" I hesitate. "All right, I'm not sure how I feel about the

181

prostitute side of things. It's kind of new territory, dating someone who occasionally gets paid for sex."

His eyebrows pull together. "So, what do you want me to do?"

It's my turn to chew my lip and fall silent. Finally, I shake my head. "I don't know. I don't really think I want you to do anything—I just need to get used to the idea."

Adrian blinks. "You... You're still going to let me do it, even if you're not comfortable with it?"

"I'm not *letting* you do anything. I want to be with you. If that's something you want to continue doing, then I'll adjust to it."

"And what if you decide it's not something you can adjust to?"

Again, I'm quiet. "Look, there's going to be a lot of stuff we run into as we go that we don't like. And we'll both have to make adjustments along the way. So, why don't we cross this particular bridge when we get there?"

He mulls it over, and after a moment, nods. "I can live with that." He starts to relax again, and trails his fingers up and down my chest. "Just so there aren't any other surprises—I sometimes forget to put the trash out, and I *always* forget to buy dishwasher detergent."

I laugh. "Okay, well, in the interest of full disclosure, I never leave my shoes in the same place twice and I use dining room chairs as coat racks."

Adrian puts a hand over his heart and sighs dramatically. "Not... Not coat racks."

"Yes. I know. It's my deepest shame."

He snorts and rolls his eyes. "Well, thanks for the heads-up. I'm sure I'll be okay."

"I should hope so."

He meets my gaze, and that soft, sweet smile comes back. As he combs his fingers through my hair, he says, "I know I said it before, but... I'm really glad you came back."

"Me too." I gather him into my arms and kiss him, and as he presses his lean body against me, I'm pretty sure the conversation is over. He opens to my kiss. We pull each other closer, and I shiver as his hand slides down and squeezes my ass.

Yeah. The conversation is definitely over.

L.A. WITT

# Epilogue
## Adrian

*About two years later.*

The sun went down an hour ago, and the Strip is crowded as always. The street is jampacked with cars, buses, and limos. Tourists and locals alike wander from casino to casino under the glittering lights, and there's the odd protester holding up a sign to let us all know we're going to hell. A typical night in Vegas.

Max and I are strolling along with the flow of traffic. We're occasionally bumped by an excited wedding party or someone who can't hold their liquor, but we're both used to that. You don't last long in this town if you can't handle being jostled by a passerby from time to time.

We just had dinner at one of the new casinos, and Max suggested walking it off before we go home. There's no destination in mind—at least, none that I'm aware of—so I'm more or less following his lead. It's only after we make a turn that I realize we're going straight toward the Bellagio. More specifically, toward the walkway alongside the fountain.

I clear my throat. "You know where we're heading, right?"

185

Max nods. He glances at me and smiles. "Yeah. I know." He checks his watch. "They should be lighting it up in a few minutes. Thought we could watch."

Well, if he's okay with going back there, I'm not going to argue.

And I guess it's not a big surprise that it doesn't bother him. It's never seemed particularly triggery for him or anything. He doesn't like talking about that short period of homelessness—though I'm sure it comes up with his therapist sometimes—but he generally copes pretty well with the fact that it happened. Hell, he's been volunteering at the homeless shelter with me since the week after he moved here.

If anything, I always expect the fountains to remind him of the week before he wound up on the streets. When he was in that room, high up on one of the top floors of the Bellagio, with a bottle of pills and a whole lot of despair.

Apparently he's okay with it, though, and we stop alongside the railing to wait for the fountains—which are currently dark—to come to life.

He slides an arm around my waist, and when our eyes meet, we both smile. I lift my chin, and he presses a soft kiss to my lips before we turn back toward the water.

Less than a minute later, the whole place lights up and the music kicks on. Jets of water shoot way up into the air, making glittering walls that rise and fall, bend and straighten. I've seen this display a thousand times, but admittedly, it's still pretty impressive.

My mind's not quite on it tonight, though. I'm too focused on the man who's standing by my side with his arm wrapped comfortably around me. Two years ago, we were strangers. Around this time last year, the sale on my place closed, and the not insubstantial chunk of change became the down payment on a three-bedroom house almost exactly halfway between his job in Henderson and mine on the Strip. I'd been a little sad to let go of the double wide I'd called home for so many years, but when we'd started actually looking at houses, I'd gotten excited, and I *loved* the place we'd bought.

Max's job isn't his dream job or anything. It's boring and sometimes tedious, but it's a solid paycheck and it's stable. He works a normal forty-hour week—occasionally fifty if things get busy—and he leaves everything at the office when the day is over. He's even started picking up some of his art again. The third bedroom in our new house has huge windows and tons of ventilation, so that's become his studio for painting.

I'm still dealing cards and stripping. We'd agreed to cross the prostitution bridge when we came to it, and it actually turned out to be a moot point. From time to time, guys still offer me money for sex, and I just…don't. When it's a choice between going to a hotel for some possibly good or possibly terrible sex, and going home to Max, it's kind of a no-brainer. And actually, he gets seriously turned on when I tell him someone made me an offer and I turned them down. It's a wonder either of us can move after those nights.

As the fountains keep doing their thing in front of us, the crowd is getting thicker. I lean into Max, and he holds me closer. We're always mindful about being affectionate in public, but right now, I don't think anyone is looking at us. Fine by me.

Being together hasn't been perfect. Not that I expected it to be. Max doesn't mind me forgetting to take out the trash or buy dishwasher detergent, but he does get kind of annoyed when I don't leave enough milk for his coffee. And I don't really care about clothes draped over chairs or shoes left in random places, but it admittedly makes my teeth grind when he leaves empty water bottles on the end tables in the living room. It's all pretty minor stuff, though. Just the annoying things that come with living together. We squabble sometimes. I can count on one hand the number of actual fights we've had, but even those aren't anything to write home about.

And speaking of home, I took him to my parents' for Christmas this past year. They *adore* him. My mom was a little uneasy about him being a decade and some change older than me, but the Max Reynolds charm won her over too. Dad liked him from the start. Maybe someday we'll tell them how we really met, but for now, *"he was playing at my table and the rest is history"* is the go-to response.

So no, it hasn't been perfect, but it's been amazing. There isn't a day that goes by that I don't stop at least once and think about how easily Los Angeles could have been the end of it. He came back, though, and I don't think I've ever been more grateful for anything in my life.

The fountains darken and the music quiets. I was so lost in thought, I apparently zoned out for the whole show. That's okay, though. Isn't like I won't see it again.

As people around us disperse, I turn to Max. "Back to the car?"

An odd little smile pulls at his lips. "Not quite yet."

I lift my eyebrows. "Okay? What do you have in mind?"

He slips his hand into mine and nods toward the planter beside us. "You recognize this spot?"

Something flutters in my stomach. I hadn't realized it until he pointed it out, but this is the exact place where I found him. The exact place I walked past, then backtracked to, even though I couldn't explain—and still can't explain—why. "Oh. Wow. I…"

"That was two years ago tonight."

"Was it really?"

He nods, and gives my hand a gentle squeeze. "That's why we're here."

I swallow. "Hard to believe it's been that long, isn't it?"

"Yeah. It is." With his free hand, he reaches into his pocket. "And it seems like this is the perfect time and the perfect place for this."

My heart stops. "Max…" I know what's coming, and I'm still startled when streetlights glint off gold. And again when Max, holding a ring between his thumb and forefinger, goes to one knee in the very same place I found him huddled against a planter.

"You saved my life. Then you *changed* it. And I want to spend the rest of it with you." He sweeps his tongue across his lips, and I wonder if he notices everyone stopping and staring as he says, "Adrian, will you marry me?"

The air is suddenly so thick I can't breathe, let alone speak, so I just nod. Because God, yes, I want to marry him. I don't even need to think twice.

Smiling, he gets back to his feet and hugs me as dozens of strangers cheer and applaud. He tips up my chin and kisses me. There might be some homophobes around us who wrinkle their noses at the sight of two men getting engaged and being affectionate, but they're drowned out by everyone else. And even those people are almost entirely drowned out by my own pounding heart. Even though we'd bought a house and have been putting together a life that's very much "us," I had no idea this was coming. Good thing he drove tonight—as overwhelmed as I am, I'll be lucky if I can walk in a straight line.

He touches his forehead to mine and caresses my cheek. "I love you, Adrian."

"I love you too." I swallow, trying to keep my composure together. "And yes, by the way. Absolutely."

He laughs and kisses me again. When our eyes meet, there are tears in his. Probably in mine too.

He glances around like he's just realizing we have an audience, and he laughs again as some color blooms in his cheeks. As they all start walking away, he cups my cheek. "Think we should head home now?"

I nod. "Definitely."

We share one last kiss in that place where two strangers somehow connected, and head back to the car so we can go home. As we walk, his fingers laced between mine, I still can't explain why that homeless man in a suit caught my eye that night.

But for the rest of my life, I'll be thanking God he did.

AT THE CORNER OF ROCK BOTTOM & NOWHERE

# About the Author

L.A. Witt is an abnormal M/M romance writer who has finally been released from the purgatorial corn maze of Omaha, Nebraska, and now spends her time on the southwestern coast of Spain. In between wondering how she didn't lose her mind in Omaha, she explores the country with her husband, several clairvoyant hamsters, and an ever-growing herd of rabid plot bunnies. She also has substantially more time on her hands these days, as she has recruited a small army of mercenaries to search South America for her nemesis, romance author Lauren Gallagher, but don't tell Lauren. And definitely don't tell Lori A. Witt or Ann Gallagher. Neither of those twits can keep their mouths shut...

Website: www.gallagherwitt.com
Email: gallagherwitt@gmail.com
Twitter: @GallagherWitt